SURGEON'S CH...

Sister Claire Tyndall's success as a nurse was undoubted—but as a woman? Richard Lynch and Dr Alan Jarvis both made it clear that they were interested in her. Both were handsome and determined, but both—unfortunately for Claire—seemed to be married already!

*Books you will enjoy
in our Doctor–Nurse series*

TENDER LOVING CARE by Kerry Mitchell
LAKELAND DOCTOR by Jean Curtis
NURSE ON WARD NINE by Lisa Cooper
SATURDAY'S CHILD by Betty Neels
DARLING DOCTOR by Hazel Fisher
THE NEWCOMER by Hilda Pressley
PICTURE OF A DOCTOR by Lisa Cooper
NURSE MARIA by Marion Collin
NURSE AT WHISPERING PINES by Elizabeth Petty
WISH WITH THE CANDLES by Betty Neels
STAFF NURSE AT ST MILDRED'S by Janet Ferguson
THE RUSTLE OF BAMBOO by Celine Conway
OMEN FOR LOVE by Esther Boyd
JET NURSE by Muriel Janes
PRIZE OF GOLD by Hazel Fisher
DOCTOR ON BOARD by Betty Beaty
FIRST YEAR LOVE by Clare Lavenham
SURGEON IN CHARGE by Betty Neels

SURGEON'S CHALLENGE

BY

HELEN UPSHALL

MILLS & BOON LIMITED
London . Sydney . Toronto

*First published in Great Britain 1980
by Mills & Boon Limited, 15-16 Brook's Mews,
London W1*

© Helen Upshall 1980

*Australian copyright 1980
Philippine copyright 1980*

ISBN 0 263 73409 9

All the characters in this book have no existence outside the imagination of the Author, and have no relation whatsoever to anyone bearing the same name or names. They are not even distantly inspired by any individual known or unknown to the Author, and all the incidents are pure invention.

The text of this publication or any part thereof may not be reproduced or transmitted in any form or by any means, electronic or mechanical, including photocopying, recording, storage in an information retrieval system, or otherwise, without the written permission of the publisher.

This book is sold subject to the condition that it shall not, by way of trade or otherwise, be lent, resold, hired out or otherwise circulated without the prior consent of the publisher in any form of binding or cover other than that in which it is published and without a similar condition including this condition being imposed on the subsequent purchaser.

Set in 10 on 11 pt Baskerville

*Made and printed in Great Britain by
Richard Clay (The Chaucer Press) Ltd.,
Bungay, Suffolk*

CHAPTER ONE

'HAD a good holiday, Sister?' Dr Mike Boyd asked the question without looking up from the notes in his hand, so Claire went on checking the drugs list without bothering to answer. She didn't feel like talking anyway, and doubted that he was really interested in her off-duty activities. 'Glad you're back,' he went on—just as Claire thought—his only concern being for work. 'Remember Richard Lynch? Damaged spine, car smash about a month ago?'

When Claire still didn't answer Mike took time to glance across at her.

'Mm,' she muttered vaguely, wishing he would at least give her time to get used to being back on duty before getting into a technical discussion.

Suddenly he grabbed her chin and twisted her face round for his scrutiny.

'Gosh, Claire, looks as if you've been on night duty for a fortnight instead of a holiday. Or was it one long orgy?'

His grey-green eyes twinkled cheekily and Claire realised how thankful she was to be back among friends.

'Let's just say it didn't work out,' she said cryptically.

'You didn't get to Spain?' he asked.

'Yes—but I'd rather not talk about it.'

Mike pinched her cheek brutally. 'Poor old you,' he managed sympathetically before returning his attention to the file again. 'Well at least you'll be glad to get down to work, so it's just as well I can offer you a challenge.'

Claire raised her eyebrows apprehensively, waiting for Mike Boyd, Doctor Extraordinaire, to take her into his confidence as she knew he would.

'Nice enough chap, this Richard Lynch,' he went on,

'but unsociable, and I want to know why.' He glanced at Claire again, evidently hoping that she was going to react enthusiastically.

'*Do* go on,' she invited politely.

'I've checked, and since his admission to Intensive Care a month ago, and during the last two and a half weeks here, he's had no visitors except the police and an insurance investigator.'

'So—maybe he was travelling incognito?' Claire suggested helpfully.

Mike glowered as only a Surgical Registrar can when he's done with being funny and expects dutiful respect.

'Sorry,' Claire muttered. 'What do you expect me to do about Richard Lynch? I must confess I can't even put a face to the name for the moment.'

Mike Boyd snapped his fingers impatiently. 'Come on, come on,' he growled. 'You're supposed to be in charge of this orthopaedic unit. Haven't you done your morning round yet?' He looked at his watch. 'Ten to nine!'

'You're early, Dr Boyd. I kidded myself that all this attention was an excuse just to see me, but as it isn't, I'm sure you'll be pleased to know that I have tended to the needs of five *very* sick patients, as well as taken the night report, *and* generally tried to acquaint myself with an ever-changing staff; never mind about new patients,' she added impatiently.

'It isn't easy,' he agreed, 'but you might *look* interested,' and with that parting shot he bounced off into the ward.

There were times when Claire felt she could cheerfully throw a heavy object at Mike, and this morning was one of them. She felt low in spirits, and not a bit as if she had been on holiday, wishing she could put the clock back two weeks and begin again.

Dr Mike Boyd was a nice enough fellow, especially on social occasions. She could always count on him to buy her a drink and come up trumps if she was in danger of becoming a wilting wallflower at hospital dances. She failed to understand why so many of the doctors went for the student nurses. Maybe they were more easily impressed. It didn't seem to matter how glamorous Claire made herself, she could never disguise the fact that she was a ward sister. She knew she had good reason to be grateful to Mike, but his devotion to duty could be a bit much at times.

She closed and locked the drugs cupboard, put the list in the basket on the floor and went after him into the ward.

Staff Nurse Jill Norris was already in attendance with the card index trolley, so Claire joined her and they toured the main ward together. Jill introduced Claire to the new patients, and Claire acknowledged the few she already knew, then she noticed that Mike was talking to a lone dressing-gowned figure sitting in a corner of the day room.

'Good morning,' she said as she intruded. 'Mr Lynch isn't it?'

The patient didn't turn round.

'This is Sister Tyndall—back from holiday,' Mike explained. 'Affectionately known to her friends as "Tyndy", but she's definitely in one of her moods this morning after the most *fabulous* holiday, so I wouldn't push your luck today, chum,' Mike added as he patted the silent patient on the shoulder. 'Don't let all that starch put you off though,' he whispered. 'There's a heart of gold somewhere in there bursting to get out.'

The head slowly turned to observe the person in question and Richard Lynch's hangdog expression momentarily lifted at Mike's frivolity.

''Morning,' Mr Lynch muttered in a dull, flat voice, and only out of courtesy.

Well, if anyone could lift him out of his depression it should have been Mike, but he'd already admitted failure, so it was obvious he was expecting Claire to make an impression.

Just then, when Claire could have followed through

with Mike's flippancy, they were interrupted by the arrival of Miss Treadgold, the head of Physiotherapy. A tall, jolly hockey-sticks type who peered round the door with a high-pitched: 'Shall we join the others then, Mr Lynch, for our daily dozen?'

Mike winced and shot Claire a despairing glance before ushering her back into the ward leaving a protesting Mr Lynch to Miss Treadgold's not-so-tender mercies.

'She would!' Mike grumbled. 'Just when he actually responded—anyway, Claire, it looks hopeful. Use your captivating charms on him—get to know him, make him feel special—find out all you can about him. We have absolutely nothing on his background.'

It was an hour before visiting time on that same afternoon before Claire had another opportunity to try her 'expertise' on Mr Lynch.

After his session in the physio class he had rested on his bed, so Claire guessed that he would be back in the day room after lunch.

Some of the more agile men were out on the lawn. It was one of those crisp but sunny spring days, welcome after a cold, snow-bound winter followed by the usual rain and floods; and Cumbria was no exception when the snow melted up on the hills and peaks, and resulted in torrents of rushing water cascading down to swamp the valleys. Most of the patients were eager to get a taste of sunshine and fresh air, but not Mr Lynch. He remained in his wheelchair alone in the corner.

'Do you like music, Mr Lynch?' Claire asked bending over him.

'What's it to you?' he snapped, without even moving.

Claire jumped back, surprise registering in her expression. Maybe he had been dozing, and hadn't heard her approach, but whatever it was it didn't really warrant such rudeness.

'Sorry, Sister,' he apologised in an undertone. 'No, I don't like music.'

'The local Silver Band is playing in the hall. Thought you might like one of the nurses to push you down.'

'If I want to go anywhere I can manage alone, but I'm all right where I am.'

'Expecting any visitors today?' Claire tried changing the subject.

He turned, his impatient black eyes penetrating hers. But he thought better of the retort ready to spring from his tongue and simply shook his head.

He sighed too, she noticed, and she got the message, clear and precise, which was: 'Go to hell and leave me alone.'

By now Claire was beginning to get over her disappointing holiday and was pleased to be back doing the job she loved. Mike was right. Having an unco-operative patient was a challenge. But that was just it—you couldn't really call Richard Lynch unco-operative. Claire had studied his file and had to admit that he did all that was required of him in the course of his treatment, but remained aloof from fellow patients, and was morose as well as being openly hostile to the nursing staff.

There had to be a reason. It couldn't be that he was merely a woman-hater, as even the male nurses reported Mr Lynch's aggressive moodiness.

Claire had made some conclusive observations by the time Mike came round next day.

'I don't intend to pander to his insults,' she told Mike indignantly. 'I mean to ignore him some of the time, and I might even be rude back to him. Give me time, Dr Boyd. I'll make him react one way or another.'

'Well, make it soon, there's a love, the new consultant arrives tomorrow and I hate admitting defeat.'

'I said *time*,' Claire replied defiantly. 'If I make it too obvious he's going to recede into his shell of silence even further.'

Mike sighed and went away. Claire felt sorry for him. He was so dedicated to his work, and eagerly took on the responsibility of consultant which the unit had been without for quite a time owing to the sudden illness of Mr Appleby, who was nearing retirement anyway. Everyone agreed that Mike did a grand job and easily qualified to take the consultancy, but once a week they sent the top man from York to supervise and now at last Mr Appleby's position had been filled, it seemed, Mike being considered too young at just thirty.

It was always a time of apprehension in any unit when a new man was appointed. Claire had precious little time to give the matter much thought, but she imagined it would be someone about fifty with loads of orthopaedic experience.

She was on the telephone the following morning early, chasing up some X-ray plates, when she heard the swing doors rock on their hinges. She half-turned at the shuffle of feet, expecting to see Mike—she did see Mike, but he was not alone. Instead, Claire's surprised stare was matched by a pair of deep-set eyes surveying her questioningly. At a glance she took in that he was quite tall, barely any difference in fact between his height and Mike's, which was almost six feet.

'Sister Tyndall, this is Mr Alan Jarvis, our new consultant,' Mike introduced.

Claire put her hand over the mouthpiece and indicated chairs in the office.

'Good morning, sir,' she said politely. 'Do please sit down, I won't be a moment.'

'I think perhaps we'll start in the ward,' the stranger stated curtly. 'Dr Boyd can introduce me to my patients as you seem to be tied up.'

Dark brown eyes, large too so that Claire seemed mesmerised by them held a look of contempt before the two doctors turned away. Mike Boyd glanced back over his shoulder with a disapproving look and the retinue of young doctors, housemen and students followed them into the ward.

'Oh, come on,' Claire said impatiently to a silent telephone, and it seemed like an eternity before a radiographer from the X-ray department assured her that the plates required would be ready in half an hour.

'Half an hour is too long,' Claire replied firmly. 'The new consultant has just arrived, so I need them within ten minutes. I'll send a nurse down.'

She replaced the phone quickly and went to break up an early morning discussion group in the sluice room.

'Nurse Harris—X-ray plates for Mr Whitmarsh as fast as you can, please. The rest of you back to work at the double—at least let's try to give the new boss a good impression.'

'What's he like, Sister?' one of them asked.

'Astute and pious from a brief glance, but that's an unfair judgment when I've only just clapped eyes on him.'

Claire turned on her heel and went after the little group of white-coated doctors. White-coated all except the new man.

'I must apologise, sir,' Claire said as he surveyed her arrival coldly. 'I was chasing up X-ray plates for one of your patients, which I hope will be here by the time you finish the round.'

'I shall need them before I complete my round, Sister,' he informed her drily.

'Perhaps we could leave Mr Whitmarsh until last, then,' Claire suggested equally as aciduously.

The alert brown eyes were coldly calculating. Alan Jarvis seemed to Claire to be just a little too cool, a little too self-assured for someone who had only just arrived.

Staff Nurse Norris handed Claire the pile of folders and escaped thankfully, while the seemingly ostentatious Mr Jarvis gave all his attention to the notes he was studying, which gave Claire time to examine him. His hair was the first thing which attracted her scrutiny. It was almost black, but on closer inspection appeared to be a very dark brown, with reddish highlights when caught in the sun as it was now. It was well-groomed and shining, not one strand out of place, which against Mike Boyd's fair tousled mop showed the difference between Registrar and Consultant.

Mr Alan Jarvis looked up, suddenly aware of Claire's critical gaze. The smooth wide forehead became instantly scored, and sleek crests above each eye almost met over his straight nose in reprehensive censure. As if reciprocating her impudent stare he indulged in a moment of assessment of her, his haunting dark eyes notably assessing her height and vital statistics, and she felt her cheeks turning pink at his mental frisking.

Being only three inches over five feet put her at a disadvantage, and as he handed her the closed file of notes she suspected that a smile was not very far away from his tightly-closed lips—lips that might have been etched from some fine work of art. Smooth and sensuous which detracted from the influence of his long, determined chin.

Only the sound of shuffling feet could be heard and all Claire needed to do was to pass him the correct file as they reached each patient while Mike gave all the explanations that were necessary.

Claire suspected that he hated this role of new boy, having to rely on Mike's information as he endeavoured to learn as much as he could about each case; but he spoke kindly to them all, and certainly succeeded in making every patient feel that he was the only person Mr Alan Jarvis was interested in at any given moment.

The wards were divided up into cubicles of four beds, and when they reached the last one there was no patient either sitting beside his bed or on it. The nurses had done well to round up all the men for the consultant's visit, but it was no surprise to Claire that Mr Lynch was missing.

Claire handed Mr Jarvis the appropriate folder after he

had dealt with the other three patients.

Mike took it upon himself to explain briefly Mr Lynch's attitude in a low voice while Claire peered through the double doors leading into the day room.

'He's in his usual place, sir. He seems to prefer being alone and in that particular corner.'

Alan Jarvis didn't glance up from the notes until he had completely familiarised himself with the case history.

'Hm,' he muttered to himself, 'let's see what we can make of him.'

Claire led the way to the far corner of the day room which looked out over a valley of trees and shrubs, flanked in the distance by green hills spattered with sheep and their new-born lambs. It was a peaceful, relaxing scene, and Claire could appreciate why Mr Lynch chose to spend most of his time there.

'Mr Jarvis is here to see you, Mr Lynch,' Claire said briskly. 'You should have been on your bed.'

'In bed or sitting in this confounded thing—what's the difference?' the injured man answered brusquely.

'Mr Jarvis has other patients to see and doesn't have time to go all over the place looking for you,' Claire scolded.

The black eyes stared at Claire resentfully, but slowly turned to the main character of the group which had followed her.

'Good morning, Mr Lynch.'

Alan Jarvis spoke brightly to the grim-faced patient, and even when he didn't get much response he continued to go into detail about his accident, and the diagnosis of his spinal injury and the subsequent treatment. Then he suddenly turned aggressively to Claire.

'Why is Mr Lynch still wearing pyjamas and dressing-gown at this time of the morning, Sister?'

Claire gulped, and glanced towards Mike Boyd for help, but he chose to turn and look out of the huge picture window.

'Most of the patients do prefer to dress as soon as they're mobile,' Claire said meekly.

'I'm not concerned with *most* of the patients. Mr Lynch is quite mobile now with the aid of his chair. Dressed like this I shouldn't think he would want to go anywhere, or see anyone. See that he gets up every morning and dresses, Sister.'

'Yes, of course, sir.' She tried to keep her voice humble but knew by the glances from the rest of the team that she had not disguised her annoyance.

As they made their way back to the office Claire heard Mike explaining about her having been away on holiday. She wished he would shut up. She didn't need him to make excuses for her.

'Coffee, sir?' Claire offered as they reached her office.

For the first time that morning Alan Jarvis actually smiled.

'That would be very nice, Sister,' he said agreeably. 'By which time perhaps the requested X-ray plates will have arrived.'

Claire went to the kitchen to organise things, and when she returned only the consultant remained. Evidently he had sent the others off to the canteen, while he had settled himself comfortably in the only easy chair, one long leg crossed at an angle over the other knee, his right hand grasped round his ankle.

Claire noticed that he was re-reading Richard Lynch's notes which she had left on the corner of her desk. Claire sat down at her desk and glanced unseeing at the nurses' duty rota.

'So Mr Lynch isn't being co-operative, Sister?' Mr Jarvis reiterated.

'He's a quiet man and apparently doesn't wish to mix with the other men,' Claire replied.

'Isn't it usual for patients to dress in their own clothes?'

the consultant queried.

'Yes—when they're well enough and able to manage reasonably easily. Like all hospitals we're grossly understaffed.'

'I like all my patients to dress as soon as it is practically possible, Sister Tyndall. It gives them a purpose, something to get up for. Women feel better for a hair-do usually, and I think our male patients should be given the same encouragement to look their best for their visitors—but apart from that for their own self-respect.'

'Yes, of course,' Claire agreed.

A young student nurse brought the coffee pot full of steaming aromatic beverage on a tray together with dainty cups and saucers, sugar, milk and biscuits. Must have everything just so for this pious consultant, Claire thought, aggrieved.

'I'm sorry, Sister—um, Claire, I believe Mike said—if I offended you by apparently taking you to task over this dressing business in front of the patient and other staff, but I did it quite deliberately. I wanted to give Mr Lynch a jolt.'

'I doubt that you succeeded, Mr Jarvis,' Claire answered quietly as she poured out the coffee.

'But I apparently gave you one,' the great man observed slowly.

'Milk, sugar?' she asked without looking at him.

'Thank you, Claire, just one sugar.'

She was forced to meet his discerning stare as she handed him the coffee. She didn't want or feel the need to reply to his observation, yet his watchful eyes seemed to be demanding some comment.

'I've been managing this unit for some time now, and no one has had cause to question the running of it before.'

'And far be it from me to question your authority on my first visit, but'—he sighed, uncrossing his legs and stirring his coffee thoughtfully—'I've had similar cases before. It can be quite hard work to get Mr Lynch's type out of his rut. But that should make your job all the more worth while, Claire. A challenge, don't you agree?'

'Yes, of course.'

My God, Claire thought, how many more times am I going to say that! Why can't I think of something intelligent to say? But her mind seemed decidedly woolly.

'Not got back into your stride yet, perhaps?' Alan Jarvis pursued patronisingly.

'In this job you have to get back in your stride the minute you walk through the door,' she retorted shortly.

The consultant laughed. He actually laughed!

'I know exactly what you mean,' he commiserated. 'After an hour or so you can hardly believe you've had a holiday. You look a nice healthy colour though—was it somewhere in the sun?'

'Spain—but it rained non-stop for the first week.'

'Then you did very well to get so tanned during the second.'

'I suppose I did,' Claire was obliged to acquiesce.

There was a lengthy pause while Alan Jarvis munched noisily on a biscuit.

'I'm not prying, Claire, but do I sense that the second week didn't come up to your expectations? What was it— poor accommodation?'

She hadn't really considered that after such a short acquaintance, and not a particularly amicable one at that, that she should divulge any details about her holiday, but at least this great man showed more interest than Mike had done.

'On the contrary—the hotel was excellent, but travelling alone was a mistake. The courier selected me to act as companion to an eccentric lady of retirement age who had every ailment the textbooks haven't listed, and foolishly I let slip my profession.'

'You had to be patient and understanding for a whole

fortnight? That was no hardship to a dedicated nurse like yourself, and I'm sure you made the most of the wild night life as soon as she had gone to bed.'

'You must be joking! Elderly ladies have a wonderful capacity for coming to life after ten o'clock, by which time I was whacked.' It was Claire's turn to laugh then.

'That will teach you to go off on your own. It shouldn't be too difficult for someone like you to find a companion, I would have thought.'

Claire wasn't sure she liked the way he said that, and she didn't answer, recognising that he was gently teasing her.

'Any more than it will be difficult to show off your special appeal to Mr Lynch,' he continued. 'I expect it's only a question of lack of communication, which I'm sure can be remedied now that you're back in your stride.'

'Lack of communication?' Claire questioned indignantly. 'On whose part, may I ask, sir?'

'Oh, not the nursing staff's, I'm sure, Claire—and you don't have to keep calling me "sir"—we're off duty for ten minutes, I think. Mr Lynch doesn't, it would seem, wish to communicate with anyone. But he's been here for over a month, so it's time his reserve was broken down.'

'He's downright rude, Mr Jarvis.'

'And Mike tells me you're going to be rude back. Coupled with a dash of your delectable charm, you should soon have him thoroughly confused.'

'I'll do my best, of course, Mr Jarvis, but I do have other patients to consider.'

'I appreciate that. Was Mr Lynch in your unit before you went on holiday?'

Claire tried to think back to before her holiday.

'I can't say I remember him, but then I had my days off preceding my holiday so I think he probably arrived as I left.'

'Have you ever considered—or do you ever visit the

Intensive Care Unit? After all the majority of those patients come to you eventually.'

'I do try to go to meet the patients being transferred, but it isn't always possible.'

'Give the matter some thought. Talk it over with Mike if you like—I believe you're fairly close—it might be worth trying to establish a relationship from the beginning.' This was Alan Jarvis at his most beguiling, Claire assumed. Charming because he wanted to start changing things the moment he had arrived, and yet he had to be cautious that he didn't upset anyone. 'Patients come into the I.T.U. critically ill, severely injured, many of them facing handicaps for the rest of their lives, so it's only natural that they form a close bond with the I.T.U. staff only to be wrenched away to be subjected to rehabilitation and completely new faces, usually within a comparatively short time.'

'We've had few problems in the past,' Claire said, determined to stick to her guns.

'That's gratifying—but perhaps a stroll through I.T.U. once a week would help both patient and staff,' he suggested.

'It's all a question of time,' Claire persisted.

'And of bending your stubborn will, Sister.' Alan Jarvis stood up abruptly, and Claire recognised all the signs of the new dominant consultant reasserting his authority.

She stood up too, prepared to walk to the door with him as etiquette demanded. She wanted to argue with him, remind him that in a position of trust and responsibility a Sister was required to have a stubborn will, but she met his hostile gaze without flinching and smiled her sweetest, sickliest smile, with an incline of her head which she guessed angered him more than any amount of argument would have done.

'I'll be around again quite soon, Sister. I don't like having regular times to see my patients. I shall drop in at odd times after clinics, and on operating days. I try to see my patients as often as possible to encourage them. Perhaps you'd make sure the missing plates are found by lunch time? Thank you for the coffee—that's another of my little whims too—I prefer to discuss the various cases with the Sister in charge in a relaxed atmosphere, so I hope you'll keep a good supply of coffee and biscuits.'

Claire followed him out of the office, and walking by his side not only felt small and inadequate, but livid that he had found cause for complaint. Then as they reached the main corridor he placed a hand on her arm, gave it a significant squeeze and said: 'I shall look forward to some speedy progress with Mr Lynch. Good morning, Sister,' and he strode arrogantly away.

Claire stood watching his departure not quite able to assess the new man as readily as she had expected to do. She turned and walked slowly back to the sluice room, and from there she mooched on to the annexe and the sterilizing room deep in thought.

Her team of nurses, all at varying degrees of progress within their general training, watched their Sister without daring to speak. Claire knew the inevitable question was on all their lips, but for some reason she could not bring herself to tell them her opinion of him.

She had always enjoyed a good relationship with her staff, and believed that for the most part they got on well together. As a Staff Nurse in a big city hospital in York she had learned that it was to everyone's benefit if she was considered 'one of them', so that petty grievances could be easily aired and dealt with promptly in order to keep a ward or unit running smoothly without petty aggravation. Now, with her experiences of being Sister for three years, she had learnt that the same diplomacy, with a touch of firm authority added when necessary, earned her the greatest respect, and encouraged each nurse to work to the best advantage within the team.

Even the most junior student nurse was made to feel a part of that team, and Claire was proud of the goodwill and happy atmosphere of her unit. Mike had been the prominent doctor for so long it was difficult now to accept a different kind of authority.

'Going to be a problem, is he, Sister?' Staff Nurse Jill Norris couldn't contain her curiosity a moment longer.

'Mm,' Claire answered vaguely. 'Young, not much experience as a consultant—likes to have his own way and enjoys trying to catch us out by popping in and out when we least expect him.' She sighed. 'Still, we've got nothing to reproach ourselves with except that Nurse Harris appears to have gone missing as well as the X-ray plates. He couldn't really find any fault with the way our unit is run, so he latched on to the fact that Mr Lynch is uncommunicative. We have to try to break down his reserve.'

'But we've tried, for heaven's sake,' Jill exclaimed. 'You can't make a man take an interest if he's determined not to. We've been trying for two and a half weeks, Sister.'

Claire held her hands up in surrender. 'I know, and I appreciate how rude he is, but I'm a new force he hasn't reckoned with, and I'll show our new boss that we don't accept failure easily, but we do a challenge.' By now several of the nurses had gathered round Claire, eager to hear her opinion of the rather dishy new doctor who had just left the ward. He was so much younger than anyone had expected, which made him the most attractive male at the Moorlands Orthopaedic Hospital and Remedial Unit.

Claire spent much of her time over the next few days giving serious thought to all that Alan Jarvis had said, but she didn't rush to make immediate changes, even though in principle she was forced to agree with his suggestions. It was all very well for a new doctor to decide that she would be welcome to visit the Intensive Care Unit to meet her future patients, but she felt it would be wise to take things cautiously; if only to wait for bush radio to bring her the rest of the staff's general opinion of Mr Alan Jarvis.

For the time being Claire had enough on her hands to try to make some sort of headway with Richard Lynch. The nursing staff saw that he dressed each morning after breakfast, and Miss Treadgold carried him through his remedial exercises daily, but when Claire did her round and tried to converse with him she came up against a brick wall every time. He wouldn't respond to small talk about a television programme, or react violently or otherwise to political gossip.

It was unusual to have a failure in a remedial unit like Moorlands, where rules were less rigid than in the ordinary hospital wards, and Claire felt she must be losing her grip. It was true that some patients took longer than others to accept their disabilities whether permanent or temporary, but when Claire went off duty at the weekend she was still no further advanced, and found herself wondering what tactics she could try next.

When she returned to duty on Monday afternoon it was visiting time. She went through the usual routine with Staff Nurse Norris and then went to the day room. There he was, just the same, as if he had never moved out of his wheelchair, been to bed, or even had meals.

It was a warm, sunny afternoon and most of the walking patients were out in the grounds with their visitors, so Mr Lynch was quite alone.

Claire purposely made a clatter with her heels and hummed lightly to warn him of her approach, then went to sit on the low window-seat in front of him.

As always he was staring straight ahead of him, into space it seemed, but his thick black lashes fanned his cheeks as he blinked at Claire's intrusion on his privacy.

She smiled. 'Hullo, Mr Lynch,' she said cheerfully.

He nodded reluctantly.

'No visitors today then?' she pursued. She didn't really expect to get an answer but he growled from somewhere low on his chest: 'You know damn' well I never have any visitors.'

'How's that, then?' Claire asked.

'I don't like people.' He was actually speaking and even lifted his head up a little.

'No, I had noticed,' Claire said, placing a cushion behind her back and settling herself against it more comfortably to let him see she meant to stay.

'Where are you from?' She refused to be put off by his sour look of contempt.

'Timbuktu,' he grunted.

Claire laughed. 'Oh well, everyone has to come from somewhere. Are your folks still there? In Timbuktu I mean?'

'I don't have any folks and you're prying, Sister, and I don't like people, especially those who pry.'

'Mr Lynch,' Claire said firmly, 'it is all part of my job to help rehabilitate you. It won't be so long before you're ready to go home for a weekend maybe. Your wife—or someone will have to learn to cope.'

Richard Lynch tore his hand over his smooth black hair impatiently.

'I'm the only one who has to learn to cope,' he growled. 'Okay? But just to satisfy your greed for gossip, there was a wife once, there isn't any more. Now mind your own bloody business,' and he swung his wheelchair round so aggressively that the arm caught Claire's knee, but he carried on out through the open double doors into the garden.

CHAPTER TWO

CLAIRE stood up and stared after him.

'Oh!' she said between gritted teeth. 'You're impossible!'

'Who, me?' Mike Boyd put his arm round Claire's shoulders affectionately.

'I know I'm not as glam as Sophia Loren, but men don't usually walk out on me,' Claire exploded angrily.

Mike let his gaze flicker over Claire's upper half.

'Mm,' he mused, 'with a little imagination and the right attire, I can see you easily in competition with Sophia Loren.'

Claire pushed him away. 'Oh, that man is really obnoxious, Mike. The welfare department will have to sort him out. I've got better things to do with my time than come begging for rudeness.'

'Don't give up, darling. You're just the one to soften him. You're doing a grand job.'

Claire rubbed her knee as together they walked back to her office.

'At least he opened his mouth,' she said to Mike. 'Said there was a wife once but now there isn't. I suppose that's something.'

'Sure, Claire—that's progress. Next time he'll tell you a little more.'

'There won't be a next time,' Claire said determinedly. 'I'm not going to say one more word than is absolutely necessary to that awful man. The ball is in your court now—you and Mr Jarvis can have the pleasure of dealing with him. You should know how to handle difficult patients.'

'But, darling, we don't have time. You're with the patients so much more than we are. You have a closer

23

relationship with them, you understand them better.'

'Not unpleasant men like Mr Lynch.'

'I bet you can do it, Claire—I'll bet you a fiver that if you really put your mind to it you can win him round,' Mike encouraged.

'If I was a gambler I'd take you on, Mike Boyd—*if* I wanted to win him round, that is, but I don't. I just want him out of my unit.'

'He has a long way to go yet. Oh, he's good with all the exercises and the swimming, but he's got to learn to walk again. Besides, so far we don't even have a next of kin, let alone an address. Now that *is* your province, sweetheart, so don't let me down.'

His lips fluttered over her cheek and Claire looked for something to hurl after the flamboyant Mike Boyd. But try as she would she could not get Richard Lynch off her mind, and during a quiet few minutes before the night staff were due to arrive, Claire went through his file of notes.

He had been brought into Intensive Care unconscious, and with extensive injuries following a car crash. Mike was right, there were no personal details included. No address, no next of kin, no religion, no occupation. It was almost as if he had come from nowhere and had as nebulous a future. This then was the key, Claire decided, but a glance at her watch forbade her to visit the I.T.U. to query his admission. Already she could hear the night staff approaching, and after she'd given her report she hurried through the corridors to the Night Superintendent's office and found Sister Miriam Hermitage on duty.

'Hullo, Mim. How are things?'

Her friend looked up from the papers on her desk and greeted Claire with a huge smile.

'Claire—you're back!'

'Have been for nearly a week, and the strain is such that I took as much of the weekend off as I could.'

'I made enquiries, and Mike told me that you were

glad to be back.'

'Not really glad to be back, but certainly relieved the holiday was over. Mim—it was a disaster.' She gave her friend a very brief version of her so-called package deal to Spain. 'The only consolation I have is that this woman has invited me to her Christmas house-party. She's quite wealthy, I believe, and lives with her brother in a large house standing in its own grounds and all that—somewhere in Wiltshire.'

'Good for you—maybe she's got you earmarked for her sister-in-law——'

'Cum-nurse and companion,' Claire put in with a laugh. 'Not on your life! I expect he's as eccentric as she is, perhaps even worse.'

'We must get together on your next days off, Claire, catch up on all the latest gossip—do the town or something exciting,' Mim suggested.

'Good idea. But the real reason for my visit now is to ask you what you can remember of our Mr Richard Lynch's admission.'

Miriam pondered, trying to recall the case, prompted gently by the little Claire knew.

'Nothing significant, and the car was so badly damaged—caught fire, I think, so that there was nothing on him to identify him, and all his belongings were lost. Can't help much, I'm afraid—he's a very reserved man, says very little, but isn't any trouble.'

'He's rude and morose, and our new consultant seems to think it's my job to get through to him.'

'Well, isn't it?' Miriam teased with a sidelong glance.

'No—but I refuse to be beaten.'

'Sorry I can't be of more help. When I do my night rounds he's usually asleep—or perhaps feigning sleep much of the time, but apart from grunts to my enquiries as to how he's feeling he simply doesn't want to talk.'

Claire shrugged. 'I know—but there are details we

should have. He must have some family, but the most I've got out of him so far is that he had a wife once, and I must mind my own—quote, "bloody business". That sort of attitude does make things very difficult but he can't stay here for ever so he'll have to talk sooner or later.'

Miriam cocked an ear as the distant sounds of an ambulance siren could be heard, so Claire left her friend to go to Casualty, and walked thoughtfully out of the back entrance, across the spacious grounds towards the staff car-park. At first she ignored a whistle, not sure whether it was human or a bird-call, but when it persisted she turned to see a wheelchair being guided with some speed along the track behind her, emerging from the shrubbery through which she had just passed.

Claire was astounded to recognise Richard Lynch, but felt convinced that it wasn't he who had whistled or wanted her, so she carried on walking.

'Sister—Tyndy—wait!' he called.

Claire swung round. 'Sister Tyndall to you, *Mr* Lynch.'

The wheelchair came to a halt at her feet—precariously close to her toes, and the intense black eyes of its occupant were glinting with amusement.

'The name is Richard,' he said calmly, 'as well you know, and you were introduced to me as "Tyndy".'

'That's only Dr Boyd's fun.'

'What's your Christian name, then?'

'Really!' Claire admonished.

'Miss C. Tyndall, Sister-in-charge,' he read from her name brooch.

'C... C... Christine? Catherine—Claire?—yes, Claire it must be, you look like a Claire.'

'How very clever of you, Mr Lynch.' She made no pretence of the sarcasm in her tone. 'What do you think you're doing out here at this time of night?'

'Spot of fresh air.'

'Then you must get it earlier in the day like the rest of

the patients,' Claire said shortly.

'I told you I don't like people.'

'The grounds are quite large enough for you to find a place on your own. The rest of the patients won't hold it against you if you don't want their company,' Claire snapped, annoyed even more at his grin.

'Going home?' he asked.

'Where else at this time of day? It is nearly eight-thirty, and once the night staff are on duty you are not permitted to leave the wards or day room. There just aren't enough staff to go around hunting for you.'

Richard Lynch grunted. 'No one will come looking for me,' he said bluntly.

'That's entirely your own fault.'

'Doubt if they'd worry if I didn't show up again.'

'You have only yourself to blame for what anyone thinks of you, Mr Lynch.'

'Why not Richard?' he asked, suddenly smiling. The sort of smile which had a bewitching effect on Claire—the kind of friendly sign that transformed Richard Lynch from being a tiresome bore to a rather handsome man for his middle-aged years. 'You call the other men by their Christian names.'

'Because most of the staff have a friendly relationship with *most* of the patients.'

He sighed deeply and tapped the arms of the wheelchair impatiently. 'I'm sorry, Claire. I know I've been beastly and I appreciate all that everyone has done for me, but I have to admit I find it irksome to be confined to this thing.'

'The quickest way to rise above your disability, Mr Lynch, is to accept it first, then you—and we—can co-operate to get you better and walking again.'

'No one can say I haven't co-operated,' he insisted. 'I've done everything that old bag Treadgold has lined up for me.'

'Not so much of the "old bag"—she's a highly qualified physiotherapist and you'd do well to persevere with her.'

'As a woman or a nurse?'

Claire felt her cheeks turning pink. She hadn't reckoned with this sudden change in Richard Lynch. 'I'll persevere with her in my rehabilitation if I can persevere with you as a woman,' he added.

'I definitely think it's time you returned to the fold,' she reproached tersely.

'I'd like to accompany you to the car-park if that's where you're heading?'

Claire shook her head. 'No way,' she said firmly. 'I am going to the car-park but you're not. You are going to turn right round and go back.'

He sat back in the chair, one arm hanging loosely over the corner edge as he eyed her intently. He had lovely bushy hair for a man of his age, really ebony, not a grey streak in evidence anywhere, and his neatly clipped moustache was a perfect match. He was still pale, his cheeks slightly hollowed, probably the effects of his accident, but apart from shadows beneath his eyes the scars of pain were fading.

'I'll go back tonight if you promise me I can walk you home tomorrow evening.'

'We'll see,' Claire said hesitantly, wondering what this man's game was. Could he be trying to find an easy way to escape from Moorlands? He didn't seem like a suicide, but then few of them made their intentions obvious.

'I'm sorry—for being so rude.' His dark eyes seemed almost liquid as he gazed up at Claire, and she found her anger melting away. 'You're right, Claire, I do have to come to terms with my condition, my lack of mobility; and the Treadgold woman says I have to learn to walk next week, and I will. I'll show you just how determined I can be. But making friends, passing the time talking about everyday topics over which I have no control and precious little interest?' He shook his head decisively. 'No, Claire—that isn't going to help me.'

Claire studied him in the growing dusk. 'You'd find your stay here so much more pleasant if you made the effort to join in some of the activities with the other men, Mr Lynch.'

'I know you mean well—and I'm sorry if I got you into trouble with this new chap the other day.'

'It was unfortunate that I had been away on holiday, but I'm sure Mr Jarvis was right. It does make you feel better to be up and dressed, doesn't it?'

'Up? That's rather an unfortunate choice of word—but dressed——' he looked down at the shabby brown trousers and checked sports jacket that he was wearing, and laughed. 'By kind permission of Oxfam. My own things were all tattered and blood-splattered after the spill, my cases and their contents burnt to a cinder.'

'Couldn't we get some things from your family?'

'Not unless you can hop across to South America.'

Claire looked at her watch. 'Let's talk about it tomorrow, shall we? Now, I really am concerned that you'll have the nursing staff sending out a search party.'

'And I'm in enough trouble already.' He reached out and held her hand, placing it between both of his with gentle pressure. 'I'll look forward to seeing you tomorrow, Claire. Goodnight.'

She watched him propelling his chair at a good pace down the path, disappearing into the shrubbery and coming out again in the far distance with a tall, white-coated figure pushing him. It was the night duty male nurse, and Claire smiled satisfactorily as she walked on to the car-park, which was situated at the side of the main hospital.

It was a very large tarmacked area divided up into various plots for the staff of the many departments, and Claire's small car was over in the far corner in the day sisters' allotted space—now the only vehicle left. In fact there were few cars remaining except in the night staff's part. But as she walked briskly along, swinging her keys, just a little complacent that at last she had made some headway with Richard Lynch, she saw that a spanking new Granada was standing in the centre of the consultants' marked area. The driver, a glamorous, dark-haired woman, started up the engine and swung round to the exit path giving the passenger, Alan Jarvis, time to study Claire, but he made no effort to acknowledge her.

She experienced a stab of dejection, and just when she had been feeling elated. She supposed that in a curious way she felt disappointed on behalf of all the unattached female staff of the entire hospital, for obviously the woman must be Mrs Jarvis.

The engine of her Fiesta turned over at the touch of the key, and she drove the short distance into town and across the small shopping centre to the modern part where her maisonette was situated. Even as she put the car away she could see the frown Mr Alan Jarvis had been wearing as the Granada had roared out of the car-park, and from now on she knew that whenever she thought of him she would couple him with the elegant woman by his side.

When he walked into her office soon after nine the following morning, Claire felt ill at ease. She couldn't describe how she felt except to say that her confidence seemed to have deserted her.

'Good morning, Sister,' he greeted curtly, and she had the utmost difficulty in meeting his stare. But he was in a businesslike manner and did his round efficiently and without wasting words until they reached Richard Lynch's bed.

He was dressed, still in the drab brown clothes he had been wearing the day before, and lying on his bed reading the morning paper.

Richard spoke agreeably to Alan Jarvis but every few

minutes stole a glance towards Claire.

'Quite comfortable, Mr Lynch?' the consultant enquired.

Richard laughed. 'As comfortable as possible in the circumstances.'

'Not finding the treatment, swimming, exercises etcetera too strenuous?'

'On the contrary—if it all helps to get me out of here it's worth it.'

Alan Jarvis turned briefly to Claire with a smile. 'I don't think Sister here will appreciate your enthusiasm for wanting to leave so soon,' he commented.

'Nothing detrimental to either hospital or staff,' Richard assured him. 'I have a great deal to thank everyone for—but for just a short while it did seem that I had little to live for.'

'When you feel like chatting up Sister Tyndall I'm sure she'd be grateful for a few details we weren't able to get down when you were admitted,' Mr Jarvis suggested.

'Like next of kin, age, occupation, religion?'

There was a hint of the old sourness and Claire inwardly cursed Alan Jarvis for trying to rush things with this patient.

'There's not much Sister or anyone else can add to my file, Mr Jarvis. I have no next of kin, no occupation, no religion—age is the only thing I'm certain of, and that is thirty-eight years.'

'No family at all?' Alan Jarvis queried.

'Not one that I talk about, Doctor, and not one that cares a hoot where I am. But if it will satisfy your curiosity I'd been working in South America for two years. I should have stayed another year, but—well—decided to come home. The car I smashed up was a hired one. I'd only just got off the plane. I had planned to get a flat or a room or something until the three-year lease on my own house is up and the tenants move out. Now I've lost my job through coming home earlier than planned, and I'm no good to anyone like this. I don't have much ready cash, and the insurance company—the accident wasn't my fault—won't pay out until I'm discharged from here. It's all one hell of a muddle.'

'You must be entitled to some benefit from the social services, and I'm quite confident that our welfare department can and will help, and advise too if you give them all the relevant facts and details.'

'Sir—with the greatest respect—there is no one I wish to see, nowhere I wish to go until I'm mobile again. Then I'm quite capable of getting myself sorted out.'

'Just as you wish of course, Mr Lynch, but I know Sister will assist in any way she can—and you are making excellent progress.' Alan Jarvis handed Claire the file, and they moved on to Mr Whitmarsh, by which time Mike Boyd had joined them.

'I'm sorry that your X-ray plates went missing, Mr Whitmarsh,' Alan apologised to the elderly man who had suffered various fractures following a fall at his home. 'It seems they've been going round to every ward except the right one, but now I'd like to show you what damage was incurred.' Mike took the plates to the wall screen and Alan Jarvis turned to Claire.

'Coffee would be nice, Sister—this is the last patient in this ward, I believe.'

Claire acknowledged his brief smile and went to her office, where the consultant's request had already been anticipated. A few minutes later the two doctors sauntered along the corridor to Claire's office deep in conversation. Alan Jarvis then took his seat in the only easy chair while Mike propped himself half on, half off the desk, one long leg swinging.

'Mr Whitmarsh will be on my theatre list for Friday, Sister. I've had time to study his X-rays now and I'm not happy—and Mike agrees with me—with his left arm. It will have to be reset.'

Claire poured and distributed the coffee then sat down

to her own, making the necessary reminder about Mr Whitmarsh.

They went on to discuss at length all the patients in the unit of four wards, Claire being surprised at the knowledge the consultant had gained about each of them in the short time he had been at Moorlands. He was observant and had a keen memory, quickly familiarising himself with patients by name.

'Mr Lynch seems to have responded to your special attention, I notice, Sister.'

Alan Jarvis had emptied his coffee cup and placed it back on the tray as he stood to leave.

'He's talking, I suppose that's a start,' Claire agreed.

'It would be wise to keep your interest on a purely professional basis, though. Don't let your charm exceed the amount required for normal duty, Sister,' he warned, then stalked off before either Claire or Mike had fully taken in his meaning.

Mike just stared at Claire. 'What's got into him?'

Claire banged her pen down on her desk in annoyance. 'Sarcastic devil!' she said angrily. 'He must have seen me talking to Richard in the garden last evening. For some reason Richard followed me. He seemed to want to talk, to apologise, and when I reached the car-park Mr Jarvis was sitting in his car about to leave. Evidently he had been watching us. He had a woman with him too—wife, I suppose.'

'Never mind him, darling. Richard Lynch is responding, that's all that matters,' and with a resounding slap on her shoulder Mike hurried after his superior.

Claire sat on, head in hands thinking. She had noticed that Alan Jarvis seemed rather formal. During previous tea and coffee intervals he had taken the liberty of calling her 'Claire', but this morning she had been 'Sister'. He had more or less commanded her to use her charm on Richard Lynch, but within days was telling her to cool off.

She visualised Alan Jarvis's view from that splendid new car—a view which would have taken in the brief scene between her and Richard Lynch. To Claire it had all been rather insignificant even though she had experienced an element of satisfaction in that the patient had responded. The new consultant was being over-dramatic, placing more emphasis on the episode than was necessary, and his insinuation that she was showing too much interest in Richard Lynch irritated her.

He was going to be a difficult man to get on with, she could tell. One minute friendly and charming, when it suited him, the next abrupt and critical. Claire sighed, trying to convince herself that she really didn't care that much whether she pleased Mr Jarvis or not. But it wasn't that simple. She had to care. He was the boss and she was responsible for seeing that his orders were obeyed, that everything ran smoothly, that the patients' welfare came first.

It niggled her for the rest of the day that Mr Jarvis had mildly rebuked her, but it was a hectic day, so that by the time she was ready to go off duty at six o'clock she had forgotten the incident, and Richard Lynch too, until she reached the path through the shrubbery and found him barring her way.

'Glad to be off duty, Claire?' he asked in a low, intimate voice. Claire experienced strange flutterings inside her. She had been in the profession long enough to be used to men making passes, and she was quite capable of handling them. It had never crossed her mind that there was a likelihood of establishing a firm relationship with a patient, though several men had tried. Claire considered such friendships unwise, remembering the advice of senior sisters not to become involved with patients. She had enjoyed the advances of young doctors, and all through her years of training had been popular with her colleagues, but once she had reached the position of Sister the dates had become less frequent, mostly because of the unsociable hours the profession demanded.

There had been one or two whom Claire would have liked to continue dating, but just when she began to show an interest the young doctor would move on up the ladder of success, and in spite of all the good intentions to keep in touch the intervening miles severed all connection eventually. Mike was the steady follower, but both Claire and he knew that the friendship was of mature kinship, typical of Plato's doctrine so that neither made demands of the other, but both enjoyed the mutual esteem and shared respect. Now Claire found herself reacting to the black eyes searching hers for a sign of compatibility.

'Yes,' she replied softly. 'It's nice to have an early evening occasionally.'

'Going home?' he asked.

Claire nodded. 'That's right.'

'Which is where?—and is there anyone to go home to?'

Claire tilted her head to one side. 'You're being very inquisitive,' she said with mock haughtiness.

Richard surveyed her with a warm, calculating gaze.

'At last I've found someone who is worth an inquisition,' he said slowly.

Claire smiled. 'You have no idea what I may be worth, Mr Lynch.'

'You'd be surprised at what I know about you, Claire. What is it—home to a lonely bachelor flat?'

Claire acknowledged this with raised eyebrows.

'Considering that you have kept your life-style a secret, Mr Lynch, I really don't see that you have any right to probe into mine.'

Richard's eyes lit up with amusement. '*Touché*,' he laughed. 'That's the appropriate reply to that I think.' Then he sighed. A long-drawn-out, despondent sigh.

'At my age there are some things one prefers not to talk about. There's nothing of interest about my past, Claire.'

He shrugged and indicated his lack of mobility. 'And in this state there's little I can do to arrange a future.'

'You can take an interest in the future, and in the present for that matter.'

'Now that does appeal to me, Claire.' His intense dark eyes bored through her outer shell so that she felt exposed—exposed to danger—exposed to his inscrutable pursuit. She felt her cheeks growing warm.

'I think you should go back to the ward,' she advised in a firm voice. 'I meant take an interest in *your* present, as well you know.'

'You're prickly this evening, Claire. That new man gets under your skin, doesn't he?'

Claire lifted her chin defiantly. 'Not any more than most doctors and consultants. This is a pretty demanding job, and Orthopaedics in particular is hard going.'

'I realise that, and I admire any girl who enters the nursing profession, especially the really dedicated ones who make it their life's work.'

'Some days are more trying than others, which is why I'd like to get home.'

Richard didn't move his wheelchair immediately, but then decided to swing it round so that Claire could walk at his side. She put one hand on the handle nearest her to help him along.

'Won't be long before I'm walking with you,' Richard said, glancing up at her.

'That's the spirit—but, of course, you don't get straight out of a wheelchair and walk. Progress may seem a bit slow to start with.'

'So the "beanpole" keeps telling me, but once I've made up my mind to do something I jolly well do it, and the sooner I'm reasonably active the sooner I can take you out to dinner.'

Claire laughed. 'You take a lot for granted, Mr Lynch.'

Richard applied the brake on his chair abruptly, and his

face had turned sour again. 'That's all you women ever say—that men take you for granted. You're never darned well satisfied. I thought I was offering you a genuine invitation, but you don't have to put yourself out on my account.'

He swung the chair round full circle and headed back through the shrubbery.

'Richard!' Claire looked after him bewildered, but he made no attempt to stop or turn round, and she knew by the speed he was travelling that he was angry.

Who was he, she thought irritably, to be angry? Hadn't he caused enough trouble already? All the same, she was sad that he had left her with such an unfriendly attitude. Slowly she turned and walked to the car-park and as she unlocked the door she kept looking up expecting to see him coming after her, but there was no sign of him. She got into her car and drove off feeling that she was the one now who had botched things up.

The traffic was heavy through the small town, and it took her longer than usual to reach her flat. She put the car away in the garage and let herself in her front door, picking up the mail that had dropped on to the mat in the small porch. She stood for a moment flicking through the letters, passing quickly over the ominous buff envelope which she recognised as being the rate demand. A curiously strange handwriting brought about a sharp reaction until she deciphered the Wiltshire postmark, then she kicked off her shoes, and went into her pleasant lounge which overlooked the green valley from the opposite side to the hospital. She curled up on the settee and opened the fine quality watermarked envelope, admiring the neat elegant handwriting which flowed across the large sheet of embossed notepaper.

Claire stopped and read the letter heading: *Karlotta*, astrologer, followed by the Wiltshire address. Then with a feeling of having been conned, she went on to discover that Karlotta had found her an interesting subject to study while they were holidaying in Spain. Absent-mindedly Claire shrugged off her coat, her cheeks scarlet from the shock of discovering that she had been unwittingly under appraisal during her two week holiday. Now she could vaguely recall a discussion over dinner one evening regarding the stars and their influence on one's life, all depending upon where the planets were at the time of one's birth. Laughingly she had confessed to being a Pisces, and had readily given away her birth date, and the time and place.

A several-page reading was being forwarded under separate cover, Claire learned from Karlotta, who hoped it would help her to find happiness and an outlet for her creative talents. The contents of the letter were such a surprise that Claire tossed it aside only half-read while she walked about her flat in a state of nervous agitation. How dare anyone pry into her character and emotions without being invited to do so? Astrology, she sneered, what a load of old rubbish that was. And she had no time for such nonsense.

Claire went into her bedroom and discarded her uniform, and slipping on a dressing-gown and slippers went to the kitchen and filled the kettle. While she waited she stood at the sink and looked out of the window at the vast open moorland. She supposed she loved the dales the more because she was London-born. It wasn't that she didn't care for city life, she did, and every now and then felt a need to join people rushing everywhere under bright neon lights; but some instinct always urged her back to the peace and solitude of Cumbria within a very short time. She loved the hazy blue of the mountain-tops, and the rich green of spring pastures as well as the sudden range of blues that met the eye of the walker when you came upon a hidden lake. Tall trees often sheltered a small village from view, with its stone walls and church spire and in winter time spiky snow-covered branches cast finger-like shadows on the smooth white carpet while a wintry sun shed pale orangey rays across cold grey waters. In every season, at any time of day, there was something to delight one's artistic senses.

The piercing wail of the kettle's whistle stirred her back to reality, and with reality the hospital and its occupants, patients and staff quickly reasserting themselves in the pattern of Claire's professional life. Richard Lynch was the dominant factor in that pattern at present. Claire knew he needed help, and both Alan Jarvis and Mike Boyd had offered him as a challenge to her.

Just when she thought she was making some headway Richard had turned on her almost spitefully, and all because she had remarked that he was taking too much for granted. An invitation to dinner as soon as he was well enough! Not much to ask, and something for Richard to work towards, but because Alan Jarvis had warned her about keeping her interest on a purely professional level she had spoken in haste with a rebuff which had obviously upset Richard. Now she supposed she would have to start again at the beginning. She felt vexed with her lack of understanding, and angry with the new consultant, whom she felt had made an unnecessarily quick assessment of her efforts, which in turn had hurt her pride.

She prepared a tray of tea and sandwiches and then opened the sliding double-glazed door in her lounge, which led to a small paved patio. A large tree-trunk served as a useful table and she sat on the small wrought-iron chair where the evening sun, trapped in the small alcove, was warm and soothing to her cheeks.

Claire took Karlotta's letter from her housecoat pocket and managed to smile circumspectly at the thought of being a suitable subject for an astrologer. One thing was certain, she decided, and that was that she would never be persuaded to visit Karlotta at her Wiltshire home now, and she was grateful that her profession was of the type to provide solid excuses.

The evening grew cooler, but it was still lovely, so

Claire changed into an old sweater and jeans, and then set about restoring her flower-beds to some semblance of order. It was quite amazing how, after months of frost and snow, the bulbs pushed their way above the ground with tender shoots. And when the shoots strengthened into sturdy stems and finally colourful blooms, Claire knew she would find relaxation in squatting on the lawn, sketch-pad on her knee and pencil in hand.

She hesitated, the small garden fork poised, as she recalled Karlotta's words concerning her creative talents. She considered she seldom had time for such pursuits, but she supposed her sketching was the outlet for her creativity. She managed to forget work as with the coming of summer she looked forward to long walks, preferably alone, so that she could sit and express her love of nature and the beautiful countryside on paper. She was lucky to have her own small flat where she had been able to turn the second bedroom into a studio for painting. That was how she filled her off-duty days in winter, bringing to life all that she had sketched and stored during the better weather.

Some people would think she lived a lonely existence, but it was sometimes a blessing after a hard day's work to go home to peaceful isolation. Perhaps she could understand Richard's preference for his own company. A certain amount of company had been forced on him through having to remain so long in hospital, so it was natural that he might need time to reflect over the past and consider his future.

Claire felt her cheeks growing warm as she recalled his quip about the present. With any of the other male patients she would have laughed off such a remark, but there had been a hint of serious suggestion in his interest in the present, with an indication that it included her. She smiled to herself, and diligently loosened the earth round the rose-bush as she wondered what advice Karlotta was going to give her.

CHAPTER THREE

ARRIVING on duty next morning, Claire had no time for even remembering Karlotta's proposed astrology reading, as she went to each of the wards under her supervision to check that all the patients on Mr Jarvis's theatre list were prepared. Operating days were the busiest of the week, and not only with the patients going to and from the theatre. Claire was aware of the ordeal such a situation created for them, however minor an operation appeared to be. She made a point of spending a few minutes with each one on the list before she did her general ward round, and she liked to be with each patient as he left the ward, though often he was drowsy and not really awake to what was happening, due to the effects of pre-medication.

While she was drinking a cup of instant coffee the mail arrived, and as there seemed to be some delay in the return of a patient from the theatre, Claire decided to take the post round as she visited each patient.

As always she was greeted warmly, and in the ward of elderly patients she gave up her time to listen to a few grumbles, but mostly reminiscences which the old folk enjoyed sharing with her. The younger nurses were helping some of them to get dressed, and already a few were sitting in the sunny day room.

It came as a surprise to Claire as she finally came to the men's ward that there were letters for Richard Lynch, but as usual he was not in the ward. She decided not to refer to the previous evening's rendezvous but be pleasant and cool, and with a cheery: 'Good morning, Richard,' she held out his mail.

His dark eyes flickered over her briefly but the letters claimed his attention as he took them eagerly.

'Hullo, darling,' he muttered, but almost as if he were

speaking as casually as any other morning. 'Seems I've been traced.' Then he glanced up to meet her gaze with a broad smile.

'It was bound to happen,' Claire said. 'The good old health service comes up trumps eventually. Anyhow, I must leave you with your post—how are you this morning?'

He seemed to deliberately evade the question as he slit open both envelopes. From one he took a Giro cheque, and from the other a quite lengthy typewritten letter with a Lloyd's cheque attached.

'Mm,' he said, raising his black bushy brows, 'it looks as if I can get out of this Oxfam garb at last.'

'Good,' Claire said, and turned to go expecting the theatre bell to ring at any moment, but Richard grabbed her wrist. His large black eyes gazed at her intently. 'Darling—I'm sorry about last night. I shouldn't have rushed off—I shouldn't have——'

'No, you shouldn't—neither should you be calling me "darling" when I'm on duty,' she rebuked sharply.

He smiled suddenly. 'You mean I can when you're off duty?'

His grip tightened round her wrist, and the unexpected violence of the contact brought a rush of colour to her cheeks.

'Let me go, Richard, please,' she begged softly. 'It's theatre day and a hectic one.'

'I know, Claire, and I appreciate that—but I was serious about that dinner date.' His grip was now infuriatingly vice-like. 'I won't take no for an answer,' he warned.

Claire began struggling, uselessly trying to prise his fingers apart with her own until he grabbed her other hand as well.

'Don't you dare call me "Claire" on the ward—and for heaven's sake—let me go,' she said angrily. For once she was grateful that he did choose to sit alone in this isolated wing of the day room, but it was not as isolated as she imagined.

'Come and talk to me when you have a minute?' Richard asked, seemingly enjoying having the ward sister at a disadvantage.

'Not if you can't behave yourself,' she answered, but the velvety smoothness of his eyes made her weaken, and she knew she wasn't hiding the natural feminine response to his attention.

'Could I see you for a moment, Sister?'

Like scalded cats both Claire and Richard broke apart, guilty eyes looking towards the doorway which framed a green-robed figure.

'Of course, Mr Jarvis,' Claire said with only a fraction of the dignity she wished she could muster.

The few yards to the door seemed to stretch into miles, and Alan Jarvis did not deflect his gaze from Claire's burning cheeks. As they walked on through the main ward neither spoke, but Claire could feel the surgeon's ebullient arrogance as he strode along in her shadow.

By the time they reached the office Claire felt as if her lungs would burst, but Alan Jarvis seemed determined not to give her room to breathe as he stood close behind her and held out a folder.

'This patient,' he said abruptly, 'Deborah Wilson—she's been in I.T.U. for nearly a week—I don't know whether you've met her——' he paused; it seemed to Claire he might be expecting an explanation as to why not, and when she refrained from answering he went on: 'I'm operating on her next, a laparotomy. Her pulse remains irregular, so I suspect she is bleeding internally. I expect a splenectomy will be necessary, then she's to come to you. Another challenge, Sister—I warn you, she is a difficult girl, but with good reason.'

Claire found she was taking a long time to recover from his sudden intrusion. She knew she felt guilty at his witnessing the scene with Richard, but hang it all, it wasn't her fault if a patient held on to her like a leech!

'We'll try to cope,' she said in what sounded a much too meek voice.

'I see you accepted and won the challenge Richard Lynch presented,' he remarked pointedly.

Claire lifted her chin defiantly. 'I wouldn't agree with you at all, Mr Jarvis,' she said adamantly. 'He is only just responding to *my* efforts at present. Soon he has to respond to the world, and that's what we have to prepare him for.'

'I'm sure you'll succeed, Sister. It looked to me as if you were making great progress. I take it that what I saw was only mild familiarity—just horseplay, mm?'

Claire's cheeks were aflame, her eyes burning indignantly.

'My Lynch changes temperament rapidly,' she informed the consultant. 'Yesterday I was convinced I was fighting a losing battle. He was quite rude. This morning he was apologising profusely, and demanding that I accept a dinner invitation as soon as he's well enough.'

Getting it all into its right perspective added conviction to Claire's words, and now she faced Alan Jarvis confidently, but the secret smile hovering around his lips only angered her. Her blue eyes blazed as she faced him, and for a moment neither flinched, and then Alan flicked her chin with the corner of the folder in his hand as he said: 'And we all know that a Sister never becomes involved with a patient. That would be most unethical—but never mind, Claire, the sooner you get him fit and walking, and discharged, the sooner you can keep your date with him.'

He turned to go, remembered Deborah Wilson and added, 'As soon as we've finished with Debbie she will be all yours, and you can use your charms on her. Maybe it will relieve the tension between you and Mr Lynch. You could try putting them together—she's a most attractive blonde—not quite as silvery as your hair, but in her more affable moments a positive little raver. She and Richard

Lynch might well be good for each other.'

Dressed in his green theatre gown and cap there wasn't much of Alan Jarvis that was visible but, Claire realised, what there was was totally in command. His eyes were dark, but whereas Richard's were black both in colour and intensity, Alan's were a rich deep brown with a melting quality, and at the moment it was Claire's confidence which was melting away.

'I shall be along later this evening to visit all the post-operative patients—probably after you've gone home,' he added.

'I don't often leave on time on theatre days,' Claire replied softly.

'Good, then I'll see you this evening,' and with a smile he departed.

The hours were too eventful for Claire to realise that her heart was singing with anticipation for the rest of the day, and even if she had acknowledged such a thing she would have put it down to her natural reaction to the patients' need of her. The ability and aptitude required to keep the running of the unit smoothly during the most exacting of days, and it wasn't until she visited the day room during an afternoon lull that she remembered the scene with Richard which Alan Jarvis had witnessed. She reflected a moment's impatience with Richard when he said: 'Did I make your heart-throb surgeon jealous this morning?'

'I shouldn't think so for one minute, but you might remember that you could be making things difficult for me.'

Richard gazed up at her affectionately. 'I'm sorry, darling, I do appreciate that you're the sister in charge of this unit, and I am grateful that I've been singled out for your special care and attention.'

'You flatter yourself,' Claire retorted. 'All my patients are special, and with their own individual needs, and you're well on the way to recovery now.'

'But unless you promise to accept my invitation to dinner, Claire, I shan't make any attempt to walk. I shall continue to stay here and make your life Hell.'

'Miss Treadgold will have her own methods of persuading you to walk, and if you persist in making my life hell I shall ignore you. Besides, we're not allowed to accept invitations from patients.'

Richard laughed. 'Come on, Claire, I'm not that naïve—it's been done before and will be done on countless occasions again. You said I would be able to get out for a weekend before I'm actually discharged.'

'That's right. Our unit is especially designed to take long-term patients who can be released for short periods depending on their circumstances and progress—and if their home happens to be reasonably near.'

'I don't have a home—it will have to be an hotel. But I can always book a double room.'

'I thought you said you didn't have a wife,' Claire said with a grin.

'You're being obtuse, Sister—my dinner invitation was to you—with a little extra private nursing, perhaps?'

'I didn't hear that, and if you pursue that line of thought you'll talk yourself into being moved.'

Richard laughed again. 'You know damned well, darling, that there's nowhere I can be moved to.'

'I understood you to say you wanted to get out of this hospital,' Claire reminded him.

'That idea is losing its appeal—let's live for the present, Claire. There's a great deal of fascination in your tender blue eyes—a lot of enchantment which I'm eager to explore.'

'You're obviously greatly improved, and I shall have to suggest to Mr Jarvis that you'll soon be ready to leave us,' Claire quipped with mock severity.

'I shall stage a relapse,' Richard warned.

'Then I shall send for two of my strongest male nurses,' Claire replied adamantly.

Richard tilted his head to one side, his expression one of amusement, no doubt because Claire was discreetly keeping her distance from his clutches.

'How come a lovely girl like you hasn't been snapped up by some unattached doctor or male nurse?' Richard asked.

'There's plenty of time, and I'm dedicated to my work.'

'You know you don't mean that—oh, I agree you're dedicated to your profession, no one could quarrel with your efficiency, Claire darling. But you don't want to be a crusty old maid, a frustrated bitch of a hospital sister any more than any other woman wants to be. Every female needs a mate.'

'There's such a thing as Women's Lib,' Claire argued.

'That's only an excuse for being left on the shelf at twenty-five.'

'Twenty-five is a nice age to be, and who said I was left on the shelf?'

'If you're twenty-five, darling, you still have time—you look younger, but I figured that you must be about a quarter of a century to have earned this position.'

Claire smoothed her apron. 'Very astute of you, but I don't see why my age is any concern of yours.'

Richard surveyed her with admiration. He didn't speak, but his fond expression captivated Claire's emotions more potently than any words would have done. She was finding it more difficult to keep this relationship on a purely professional basis. She had only been doing her job in getting Richard to respond, but now his response was becoming too personal for her to ignore. But ignore it she must. She knew that whatever her personal feelings were she must strike that intermediary balance of adroitness coupled with friendly interest, but with a man of Richard Lynch's attractive qualities she knew it was going to be difficult.

47

She turned on her heel, knowing that he was well aware now of the effect he had on her, and on her way back to her office she met Mike Boyd.

'Hullo, Mike—how's it going? The list can't be finished already?' she said.

'No, not yet but we're in good time, only a couple more to do. The boss will be round later, but as it's my tea break he suggested I call in to see how our Debs is.'

'She's commanding a great deal of attention from Sir,' Claire remarked.

'And she'll command a great deal of *your* attention, sweetheart, when she recovers from the op.'

'She's very quiet at present. I was there when she came round from the anaesthetic, but she went off to sleep again almost immediately. I've had no complaints from the nursing staff on that ward.'

'I can't promise that you won't ere long,' Mike cautioned.

They walked side by side chatting until they reached Ward Two of the orthopaedic unit.

'She threatened to cause a rumpus if Alan moved her to an ordinary ward—*she* considers she is too ill to be moved out of I.T.U.'

'Oh dear—one of those. How old is she, then? I took her to be in her teens.'

'A randy young eighteen, Claire—a spoilt brat at that, but Alan doesn't see it that way.'

'Teacher's pet, is she? Mr Jarvis rated her as "a positive little raver" in her more affable moments.'

'You can say that again—keep the male nurses well out of her reach.'

The junior sister of the ward emerged from behind screens as she heard footsteps.

'Everything all right, Sister Cannon?' Claire asked. 'Dr Boyd would like to see Deborah Wilson.'

Tricia Cannon, a short, stocky, happy-go-lucky girl

with mouse-coloured bouncing curls held up two crossed fingers as she led the way to the end bed.

'All's quiet at present, Sister—she woke long enough to say that she felt shivery, asked for a drink and in the next breath was so hot she wanted to throw off all the bed-clothes, but she quickly drifted back to sleep again.'

Mike and Claire perused the chart hanging at the foot of the bed.

Deborah Wilson looked young and sweet with her fair lashes moist on her rosebud cheeks. Her temperature was raised but that was to be expected during the post-operative period.

Mike sighed as he replaced the chart. 'I can only report back that she's sleeping satisfactorily,' he said.

'What did Sir expect so soon after the operation? Even Miss Wilson can't be capable of seducing anyone at this stage, for heaven's sake.'

Mike smiled down at Claire. 'Don't you believe it—you just wait until you see what she's capable of.'

'And she was in I.T.U.?'

Mike nodded, and together they returned to Claire's office. 'Upset that department well and truly, so Alan decided to operate sooner than he intended so that she can be moved to an ordinary surgical ward.'

'Sounds as if she'll be going home as soon as she's fit enough.'

'Unfortunately things look very black for her, with both parents still in I.T.U. Their car was in collision with a tanker on the motorway.' Mike placed his hand on Claire's shoulder. 'Any chance of a cuppa? I haven't time now to go to the canteen.'

'You should make time, Dr Boyd. Everyone's entitled to their breaks.'

'I know,' Mike said wearily, flopping into the easy chair, 'but I'd prefer to get back. It's a pleasure to watch the master at work.'

Claire called to a passing nurse to fetch the tea and then raised her eyebrows at Mike.

'That's praise indeed from someone who's been doing the job single-handed for weeks.'

'I'm enjoying the refresher course—honestly, Claire, Alan Jarvis is a wizard in Orthopaedics.'

'But not with randy teenage girls?'

'Funny that—I mean I don't know why he should treat her as extra special—all *his* patients are special. I suppose in a way she's temperamentally difficult just as your Richard Lynch is. I hear he's making excellent progress.'

'As far as I know he has been doing that for as long as he's been at Moorlands, apart from the initial concern at the beginning. He's still moody, but certainly more communicative these days.'

'Only with you, though?' It was half a statement, half a question which Claire didn't answer except by a fluttering of eyelashes and a faint blush creeping into her cheeks.

'Be careful, sweetheart,' Mike added. 'I asked for your help, offered you a challenge, but I didn't suggest you should fall head over heels in love with the man.'

'I'm not likely to do that. Men have made passes before you know, Mike.' But Claire was forced to drop her gaze demurely at the suggestion.

'I suppose they must have,' Mike said thoughtfully. 'But you're considered the stable, reliable kind of girl who always has both feet firmly on the ground.'

'And what has happened to change your mind about that?' Claire questioned cryptically.

'Nothing—only—well—you know, our male patients are usually in groups, and that's safer for horseplay than a lone man who prefers his own company making advances. Don't get involved, Claire, forget I suggested you should try to win him round.'

'He'll be walking soon, and then he'll be moving on.'

'And you know that as he doesn't appear to have home

or family in this country, we can't just push him out on the streets,' Mike affirmed.

Thankfully the tea arrived, so Claire avoided continuing the conversation. Mike took the last remaining cream biscuit and drank his tea noisily. Then just as he was about to rush back to the theatre he paused in the doorway.

'How are you fixed next Sunday week?' he enquired.

Claire looked from Mike to the duty rota pinned above her desk.

'I'm working all this weekend—off the following Saturday afternoon and all day Sunday.'

'That's splendid. I can put your name down then for a fell walk, can't I?'

'Gosh—don't I do enough walking here?'

'No,' Mike stated emphatically. 'You need to get out in the fresh air, right away from the hospital.'

'Like going walking with some of the staff?' Claire scoffed.

'Oh come on, sweetie, you haven't got anything else lined up so what's the matter with your colleagues?'

'Nothing—absolutely nothing,' Claire said light-heartedly.

'I'll put your name down—Miriam's coming too.'

'I'd like to think about it, Mike. See how I feel nearer the time,' Claire insisted.

Mike waved a warning finger in her direction.

'Then you'll be lazy and stay home with your feet up. Your name will be on the list by this evening. I'll give you details later on—well—it'll be on the board. See you, Claire, thanks for the tea,' and he hurried away, and from a distance Claire could hear his bleeper going.

She smiled wistfully to herself thinking back over Mike's words. Stable, reliable—ugh; she shrank from such a description. How uninteresting she must be. No wonder Mike only invited her anywhere when there would be plenty of others around too. Perhaps she should try to be a little more frivolous, especially when in the company of men? But that resolve was quickly forgotten as post-operative patients in all four wards demanded attention as they came round from the anaesthesia. She was still going from ward to ward when she collided with a dark-suited figure at the entrance to Ward Two.

'Ah, Sister Tyndall—still busy I see?'

Claire found herself at a loss for words as the not unpleasant tang of cologne reached her nostrils. Alan Jarvis looked immaculate in his charcoal pin-striped suit. His jacket was undone to reveal a matching waistcoat as he stood surveying her with one hand in his trouser pocket.

His recent activities of completing his list for the day, followed by a shower, flashed vividly through Claire's mind as a silent voice urged her to condescend to the consultant's distinguished appearance.

'They all seem to come round at once,' she answered a trifle lamely.

Was he all dressed up and dashing off to meet his wife? Claire refused to dwell on the fact that the beautiful woman driver of the Granada was indeed a lucky woman, even though she knew it to be true.

'I'll see them all, Sister—shall we start in Ward One?' he suggested affably.

'Yes—yes, of course—may I?'

'Do finish whatever you were rushing off to do.'

Claire quickly found Staff Nurse Norris, who took the prepared syringe to Mr Whitmarsh, and Claire returned to Ward One.

Few of the patients who had undergone surgery felt like talking, but Alan Jarvis made a point of visiting each one to ask if they were reasonably comfortable, and in every case he explained in detail to Claire exactly what he had done.

She had always liked theatre work even if she hadn't made it her speciality. Now she enjoyed listening to Chief

Surgeon Alan Jarvis, and without realising it, and without embarrassment discussed each patient with him. Together they became dedicated partners, their immediate interest only in the men and women of varying ages in their care.

When Claire made a vital observation regarding a male patient with multiple fractures, Alan suddenly paused, and glanced down at Claire intently.

'You really do know your stuff, don't you, Claire?' he said.

His voice was warm, barely audible, certainly not to anyone near, and Claire realised that she had impressed him. She hadn't set out to do so. This was her profession as well as his, and it was her job to know even the most seemingly unimportant detail about every patient, and she loved the challenge her work gave her. She welcomed the fellow-feeling between them and smiled easily.

'And if I may say so, sir, you seem to as well.'

He answered with a rare intimate smile, inclined his head a little and whispered: 'Team work, Sister—that's all it needs to keep the unit running efficiently.'

Some minutes later they moved on to Ward Two and eventually the end bed where Debbie Wilson was moving restlessly.

Alan smoothed her forehead with long, skilful fingers and she opened her eyes.

'Hullo, Debbie—back with us again, then?'

She rolled her eyes, apparently trying to focus, and then endeavoured to move higher up in the bed to ease her breathing.

'How do you feel?' Alan asked kindly.

'Hot and uncomfortable. Where am I?—and who's *she*?'

Her big green eyes were focussing now, and openly hostile towards Claire.

'Sister Tyndall, and she's the sister-in-charge of the whole unit of four wards. She's a specialist in Orthopaedics and remedial work, so you're in very capable hands.'

'Hullo, Debbie—that's the worst part over, so now all we have to do is to get you up and about,' Claire said agreeably.

'It may be the worst part for you, but not for me,' Debbie answered aggressively. 'I wanted to stay with Mum and Dad, that's where I should be—but *he* won't let me.'

'The Intensive Care Unit is where patients come to have the initial special care they need following accidents, Debbie, as I've told you before,' Alan explained. 'We can only keep them there until we've made an assessment, and in your case an operation was necessary. That we've done, and you now come automatically to a surgical ward where you'll receive the specialist nursing you require.'

'How will I know what's happening to Mum and Dad?' she asked gloomily.

'You can always ask me when I come round to see you, or Dr Boyd, or, of course Sister Tyndall or the sister in charge of this ward—um, Sister Cannon isn't it?'

'Don't like her—she's bossy,' Debbie complained with a pout.

'Debbie, my dear, you have hardly been here long enough to make such an accusation, and if you're going to be unco-operative and unpleasant then the nursing staff will have every right to be bossy. And,' he added, straightening up and placing his hand gently round her chin, '*I* shan't bother to come and see you again.'

Claire noticed the chin quiver slightly and the huge green eyes became moist as Debbie blinked back tears.

Alan bent closer to her again and wiped away the first trickling one with his finger. 'Be a good girl for me, Debbie,' he persuaded softly. 'I'll write you up something to help you sleep, and I expect I shall see you briefly tomorrow.'

Claire could see that Debbie had put up a good fight to

be on the defensive, but the after-effects of the anaesthetic were making her weepy, which was usual. Debbie held on to Alan's hand desperately for a moment, and then he pulled away and walked on to the next patient.

Outside in the corridor later, Alan wrote up the necessary sedatives to suit the various patients and with a sigh handed the prescription pad to Claire.

'Poor Debbie, I'm afraid she's in for a rough time,' he said, then at Claire's questioning frown he continued: 'Debbie's injuries are not that serious, as she was travelling in the back of the car. I'm glad I did a laparotomy which proved, as I suspected, that the spleen was damaged. With that now removed she should make good progress, but both her parents'—he sighed and shook his head—'it's going to be a miracle if either one of them survives.'

'I'm so sorry—poor Debbie,' Claire said with feeling.

'We've just got to keep fighting for them both, but'— he looked deep into Claire's eyes—'you go along to I.T.U. and see for yourself. Mrs Wilson is still unconscious but talk to her, tell her that Debbie's fine, have a chat with her father too. Will them to live, Claire, for Debbie's sake. She has no one else.'

Claire felt a little guilty after Alan had said goodnight and left, and she also indulged in a little pique that he had found it necessary to remind her again of his suggestion to visit the Intensive Care Unit. She looked at her watch and hurried to her own office where she knew she would find the night staff waiting to take the report.

Miriam arrived when she was halfway through and listened intently as Claire ended the report with her own personal observations about the more complicated cases. It had been a hectic day, and she was ready to go to the peace of her own flat. It was useless to go to I.T.U. at this hour, she excused, and for a fleeting moment wondered whether Richard was patiently waiting for her in the garden.

Miriam broke into her thoughts.

'You look tired, Claire. Off you go—we're quite capable of coping. Mr Jarvis was right to move Debbie Wilson, if you're thinking it was a bit callous of him. She was being a nuisance.'

'How?' Claire asked.

'Demanding attention, mostly when it was needed more by her parents.'

'She's frightened, Mim, she must be,' Claire said. 'For a few days now she'll feel sorry for herself, so perhaps she'll settle down.'

'Her parents really are in a bad way, and she's going to have to be told.'

'That's up to Mr Jarvis. I'm sure she puts up this defensive front to hide her deeper feelings.'

'Go on, you old softie, you're off duty now, I bet you haven't had any time off today?' Mim taunted her friend.

Claire shook her head. 'No—but then I seldom do on operating days. I like to see all my flock safely back.'

'And when you've knocked yourself up they won't be *your* flock. I hear Mike's twisted your arm to come fell-walking on Sunday week.'

'He's put my name down, but I haven't decided one way or the other yet.'

'It'll make a nice change and the weather is promising.'

Claire laughed. 'You're an incurable optimist, Mim, it can change several times between now and then. You can't really expect this sunshine to last for over a week.'

'I'm looking forward to it—heaven knows the winter has been long enough. We needn't walk all the way with the others, we can stop off and enjoy a chat while we rest.'

'I'm not committing myself at this stage,' Claire said.

'You've been committed already. Mike has put both our names on the list, with two loaves of sandwiches by mine and savoury pastries by yours.'

'Oh, that man!' Claire exploded. 'He really has got a cheek.' She picked up her bag and cape, and Miriam walked to the double doors with her where they parted.

She felt a curious lilt in her step as she walked through the grounds. Could it be that she was actually pleased at the prospect of Richard waiting for her in the shrubbery?—but as she emerged on the other side and there was no sign of him she found herself glancing over her shoulder, feeling slightly disappointed.

He was much in her thoughts as she drove home, and as she ate a light meal only half concentrating on a television programme she found herself reliving the day's events. The contact with Richard, the chat with Mike, the image of Alan Jarvis. Confused and conflicting thoughts continued to harrass her loneliness. It was after a busy work-filled day that she noticed how empty her personal life was. She tried to visualise having a man to come home to, a man to discuss the day's problems with, a man to soothe and caress her when she was tired.

Which of the three men who sprang to mind was eligible to fill her needs? she wondered. Mike was fun, when he wasn't over-working, but not really on her list of suitable mates. Alan Jarvis was already spoken for—married to the beautiful driver of the new Granada. Vehicle and driver alike, Claire mused, passenger too, sleek, polished and smooth-running. She allowed herself a moment of idyllic imagination. Who wouldn't be flattered to have a man like the devoted consultant to come home to?

But such impossible dreams quickly faded as the third member of her list reasserted himself in her priorities. Richard made her feel that she mattered as a woman, mattered to him, and she found herself visualising him, fully recovered, dressed as immaculately as Alan Jarvis, looking into her face with undisguised desire in those evocative dark eyes.

Could it be that at last she was falling in love?

CHAPTER FOUR

Long after Claire had retired to bed, Richard Lynch dominated her thoughts. She realised that his flattery gave her a boost. In turn the mild flirtation was giving Richard a reason to work at his recovery. Claire had to remind herself yet again that he had never needed to be encouraged, as he was one of the most co-operative patients they had ever had, considering the seriousness of his injuries. It was simply that he had been reticent to join in the general activities of the ward. She knew from the report that he enjoyed doing exercises in the special gymnasium, and gave no trouble during his daily swim in the cleverly devised apparatus, but he did refuse all invitations to watch television, or play cards with his fellow patients. It seemed fairly obvious to everyone that there were problems on his mind that he was endeavouring to sort out alone.

What did anyone really know about him? Only that he had been working in South America and had come home earlier than scheduled. Claire knew that the secret of his self-inflicted segregation must lie in the reason he had felt it necessary to break his contract. If only she could dissolve the barrier of silence, she was convinced he would be a happier man. Since she had gained some headway with him she felt that he was less bitter, but there was his future to consider, and that, as well as his past, were the things he simply refused to discuss. The present he had said was what mattered most. Probably that was his way of telling Claire that all he wanted was a temporary friendship to help him through his stay at Moorlands. She should accept it as a compliment that he had responded to her, but she knew that it meant much more to her, however hard she tried to heed the warnings of Alan Jarvis and Mike Boyd.

Perhaps they and Mim were right in that she needed to get out more, away from the pressures that her unit forced upon her. The fell walk sounded like fun. It was only at hospital dances or in the canteen that she ever met any of the rest of the hospital staff, so such an outing would provide a good opportunity to expand her circle of friends. She would take her sketch pad, and as she closed her weary eyes she could conjure up the green hills rising above craggy moorland, mountain passes and waterfalls, valleys and lakes and the calm serenity of such outdoor bliss quickly carried her into a dreamless sleep.

She slept until much later than usual, secure in the knowledge that she was not on duty until ten a.m. next morning, and on reaching her office learned that Alan Jarvis had been and gone. She was quickly into the swing of the usual routine, and fitting in a visit to each ward, leaving her own, the busiest and largest male ward until last, found that several patients had gone for remedial treatment, Richard Lynch among them.

It was much later in the day, during afternoon visiting in fact, when Claire managed to go in search of him again.

The weather was still good, so that patients and visitors were scattered over a large area of the beautiful grounds of Moorlands. It was Claire's intention to spend a few moments with Richard as well as other patients who for various reasons did not have visitors. She combined this with writing out medical certificates and dealing generally with patients' requirements.

As usual Richard was sitting in his wheelchair, not near the window but facing a blank wall.

'Hullo, Richard,' Claire greeted cheerily.

He didn't speak or move, and when Claire went to

peer into his face she was able to appreciate the transformation which had taken place over the last couple of weeks because now, almost overnight it seemed, he had reverted into his own private world of exclusion.

'I said "Hullo",' she persevered.

'So? What do you want me to do about it? Kiss your feet?'

'Richard!' It was then that Claire noticed two walking sticks lying across Richard's lap. 'Ah!' she said, immediately sympathetic to his frustration. 'Have you been having a go?'

'If you mean has that stupid bitch been trying to teach me to walk again—yes—and it isn't going to work. I can't do it and that's that.'

'Richard.' Claire's voice was full of understanding. How many times had she heard those words from disheartened patients before? You'll do it, honestly you will,' she assured him. 'It won't happen in five minutes, it will take time, but bit by bit your confidence will grow.'

One stick hurled aggressively into space just missed her, the other one fell wide and clattered beside the first on the floor.

'Bloody stupid women—leave me alone, the lot of you,' he barked.

Claire could feel her heartbeats resounding wildly, and had to admit if only to herself that she was just a little afraid of Richard Lynch in one of his black moods. His handsome features were stripped of elegance, and in its place were lines of disappointment. Afraid or not, she did understand and oh, how she felt for him.

'I know how despondent you must be feeling, Richard,' she said softly. 'You were expecting a miracle and it didn't happen. But it will in time. I only wish there was more I could do to help.'

'Help!' he roared at her. 'You helped all right. My God, you women can turn on the charm when you want to. Wanted to chalk me up as one of your successes, I suppose—well you can damn' well see what a failure I am.'

His fist came down on the arm of his chair so hard that he must have hurt himself, and with head burrowed into the collar of his jacket and without glancing at Claire he propelled the chair around to go off, but Claire put out her foot and stopped him. For a moment she thought he intended to continue over her foot, but he lifted his hooded dark eyes long enough to see the sadness in Claire's.

'Darling,' she whispered imploringly.

An equal measure of shame and guilt forced him to hang his head.

Claire noticed his knuckles turn white as he gripped both arms of his chair, then with a sigh he pressed the knuckle of his forefinger to his mouth.

'Try to be patient, Richard, please,' Claire begged. 'You've been so marvellous all along.'

He looked up suddenly and black eyes gazed into pale blue ones with a look of scorn.

'Don't patronise me, Sister. I've been a confounded tyrant to you all,' he admitted savagely.

'You know that isn't true, Richard. You could have been more friendly, but no one could fault your efforts at fighting back. And you'll win—you really will.'

Still gazing directly at her he sighed heavily. 'I know you mean well, Claire—but, oh, God, do problems never cease?'

The anguish in his voice tore at her heartstrings.

'Darling—will you let me help you? When it's quiet—like now—will you?'

'No, Claire. I can't bear you to see me like this—a helpless wreck.'

'You're not helpless and you know that. It's my job, Richard. I'm used to seeing people much more handicapped than you, and I'm proud of my profession when I see them walk out of here unaided, fit and well.'

'I shall never do that,' he muttered.

'You will, you know. You've jolly well got to or that dinner date is off.'

After a long pause his lips parted in a gentle smile. 'You're a super girl, Claire.' He reached out to place his hand over hers still resting on the arm of his wheelchair. 'If only things could be different, if only I hadn't already made a mess of my life. But I have, and I'm not going to mess up yours.' He looked so pitifully sad, his dark brows almost shielding the eyes which were a mirror of his mood.

'Of course you're not, and you're going to get yourself sorted out. Sitting here brooding isn't helping, Richard. Do you feel like trying to stand? Will you have a go with me?'

He placed the palm of her hand against his lips.

'That's the sort of improper suggestion I've always been able to follow through, but if it's walking we're talking about, not any more today, Claire. It's not the effort of trying to balance which has tired me, but the defeat. Perhaps a few more times on Miss Treadgold's contraptions will help.'

'One step at a time, Richard, and in a couple of weeks you'll have forgotten you were ever confined to a wheelchair.'

'If each step takes me nearer my dinner date with you, darling, it won't be for the want of trying.'

Claire squeezed his hand as she saw a junior nurse coming through the main ward.

'I'll come back later to do your certificate. You're due for one this week, aren't you?'

'Make it soon,' he whispered, and Claire went to meet the nurse.

'The sister on I.T.U. said would you phone her back

please, Sister.'

'Thank you, Nurse, I'll do better than that, I'll go to see her personally.'

Claire explained to Staff Nurse Jill Norris where she was going and took the lift up to the next floor. She found Sister Burgess at her desk in the small office. She looked up and a look of mock dread came over her face.

'No—I will not have Debbie back,' she said emphatically.

Claire laughed. 'I wouldn't dream of suggesting such a thing. I thought you wanted me.'

'Yes, Tyndy, but you needn't have come up—I mean I'm pleased to see you, but it was only to tell you to prepare for Debbie's father. Hope you've got room for him?'

'I think we're losing about three tomorrow—will that do?'

'Admirably. Mr Jarvis thinks it might help Debbie if her Dad is not too far away, and they can sit together in the day room then.'

'Sounds as if that will make life easier for us, but is he well enough?'

'He did seem much improved this morning, but his wife is still unconscious.'

'Mr Jarvis asked me to come and get to know my future patients. He suggested I should talk to Mrs Wilson.'

'We're trying that technique all the time. Mr Jarvis is hoping both Debbie and her father will get well quickly so that they can sit and talk to her.'

Sister Burgess, a middle-aged, kindly woman, stood up and led the way into the almost quiet reverence of the Intensive Care Unit. In hushed tones as she visited each patient, checked the equipment and machines, she explained about each one to Claire who knew that a small percentage would probably never reach her remedial wards, and Mr Wilson had been one of these as well as his wife, but now he was taking an interest in all that was happening.

'This is Sister Tyndall, Mr Wilson. She's the Sister-in-charge of our remedial wards where Debbie is now.'

Claire explained the type of surgery which had been necessary for Debbie to undergo, and assured him that she was making good progress, promising him that he would see her when he was moved down to the men's ward.

'He seems too humble a man to have a difficult daughter like Debbie,' Claire said afterwards as they returned to the corridor.

'That's probably the trouble—they've spoilt her outrageously.'

Claire was able to get a better idea of the Wilson family from Sister Burgess before she could make her own judgment during the subsequent few days.

Debbie Wilson quickly recovered from her operation, the enforced rest enabling the bruising she had sustained in the accident to heal easily, but with progress she became demanding, and the nursing staff were constantly complaining of her behaviour.

'She really does try the patience of a saint,' Claire reported to Alan Jarvis when he appeared unexpectedly, late one morning.

'I did warn you, Sister,' the consultant said wryly. 'What's she been up to now?'

'Refused to dress—or rather dress herself, which she is quite capable of doing now. I explained we were too busy to help her this morning and that if she couldn't manage alone then she couldn't go to see her father.'

'And?' Alan Jarvis prompted, obviously expecting some abnormal reaction.

'She threw a garment of clothing at each nurse as they passed, the final one at me which landed on the medicine trolley.'

'What did you do?'

'Threw it back at her.'

Alan smiled. 'Shame I missed the fun.'

'When we're busy, Mr Jarvis, it isn't fun,' Claire stated firmly.

Alan raised his eyebrows in acknowledgment. 'Who else isn't behaving?'

Claire sighed, and gave him the run-down of most of the patients in all the wards.

'And Mr Lynch?' Alan queried.

'Not very pleased with life, still unsociable,' Claire informed him, trying to sound indifferent.

'What have you been doing to him?'

'Nothing—it's not my fault that he can't walk miraculously after two months in a wheelchair.'

'Thought he was just going to get up and walk off, did he?'

'Apparently.'

'Pity—if he feels despondent about it, I mean. He seemed to be so much better, responding so well.'

'I offered to help, but he threw his sticks at me the first day.'

Alan studied her for a moment. She felt a faint blush creeping into her cheeks, but she had hoped that by telling Alan Jarvis of Richard's frustration he would realise that she had not taken her interest beyond the call of duty. She didn't continue to enlighten Mr Jarvis as to the intimate conversation which had followed.

'I'm sorry if they all take it out on you, Sister Tyndall. I'm sure it's nothing personal. Let's go and see if anyone will enact their revenge on me.'

He walked close beside her as they visited each patient, and in Ward Two he came to a halt at the foot of Debbie Wilson's bed. Propped against her pillows, her arms folded, she remained quite still as she peered scornfully from the only available eye. Her head and the other eye were obscured by a pair of cotton floral briefs which had stayed exactly where they had landed when Claire returned them to her.

'New fashion, Miss Wilson?' Alan enquired with a smile.

'*She* threw them at me,' Debbie accused bluntly.

'Sister Tyndall has an excellent aim. Do you play darts or some other exacting sport, Sister?'

'The only kind of sport I have time for, sir, is verbal fencing,' Claire said in a sudden fit of ill-humour.

Alan didn't take his gaze from her face. Claire didn't really know why she had made such a remark, hinting that she had a grievance against him, and she couldn't think of anything to say now which might make things better, but the brief silence was shattered as the cotton briefs whizzed through the air towards Alan Jarvis. With little effort he caught them, and turned his attention to Debbie.

'Stop making eyes at *her*,' Debbie commanded. 'You're supposed to be visiting me.'

Alan casually strolled to the side of the bed.

'Young lady,' he said sternly. 'I will make eyes at whom I choose, and it will certainly not be you until you are decently dressed and better behaved.' He placed the briefs beside her and turned to leave.

To Claire's utter astonishment Debbie peeled off her dainty, frilly, apricot-coloured nightie and threw that at Alan.

'Well, aren't you going to examine me?' she invited provocatively.

Claire started to pull the curtains round to screen Debbie.

'No, Sister—if she chooses to make an exhibition of herself, then let her.' Alan walked slowly back to Claire and put the nightie in her hand. 'Now, Sister, who have we got that really needs my attention?'

'I do! I do!' Debbie screamed and when Alan took Claire's arm and led her out into the day room Debbie's screams turned into passionate sobs.

'Ignore her, Claire. It's the only way,' Alan said softly, and when he'd talked with all the patients sitting in the sunlit day room he passed through the door which led into the recreation room of the men's ward. Here he talked and joked with the male patients, most of whom were well on the way to being discharged, then he moved on into the ward where Mr Wilson was dozing but responded to Alan's visit enough to ask after his wife and daughter.

'No change in your wife, I'm sorry to say, but Debbie is making excellent progress. If you feel up to it she can come and visit you later on today.'

'That would be nice,' Mr Wilson managed to say, and Alan continued on his round, visiting the remaining patients who were not at remedial classes.

'Let's go back and see what havoc Debbie has wrought.' He took the nightie from Claire's arm, and together they sauntered back the way they had come.

Debbie had pulled the sheet up round her and was crying bitterly, probably because no one was taking the slightest notice of her.

Alan deliberately paused halfway down the ward and stopped to discuss various cases with Claire, then, as if he had all the time in the world strolled to Debbie's bedside. He observed her silently.

'I want my nightie,' Debbie muttered into the sheet.

Alan motioned to Claire to draw the curtains round the bed and almost before she was completely screened Debbie threw herself at Alan, clasping his neck tightly, pressing her face against his.

'I want you to like me,' she sobbed.

Alan struggled to release her hold.

'No one likes precocious children,' he told her firmly.

'I'm not a child, I'm eighteen.'

'And very immature. You may find yourself in a situation you can't handle if you go around discarding your clothes, Debbie, but you don't impress me,' he told her sternly.

'Then why don't you take any notice of me? You're always talking to *her*!'

'Sister Tyndall doesn't throw things at me, and we do have to discuss the running of the ward. I told Sister you were a good girl, Debbie, but I'm ashamed of your behaviour this morning.'

There was a long pause before Debbie said: 'I want to see Mummy.'

Alan was thoughtful too for a moment before he answered: 'She's critically ill, Debbie.'

Slowly, Debbie raised her tear-stained cheeks and looked helplessly at Alan with large, frightened eyes.

'Is she—can I——?'

Alan shook his head. 'I can't tell you any more than that, Debbie dear, I wish I could. Your father is improving, I'm pleased to say, and has been transferred to the men's ward right next door. If you're sensible, and get dressed and do what you're asked to do willingly, then Sister will take you along to sit with him. He's looking forward to seeing you.'

'But Mummy?'

Alan slipped the flimsy nightie over Debbie's head and she meekly pushed her arms through the elasticised sleeves.

'You could help your mother, Debbie,' he suggested gently.

'How?'

'If you were very sensible you could sit by her side and talk to her.'

'Is she conscious now, then?' Debbie asked eagerly.

Alan's expression was grave and Claire didn't envy him

the difficult task he had to do. He shook his head sadly. 'No, and I'm afraid she may not even hear you, Debbie, but we believe in trying to persuade her to come back to us.'

'She's going to die,' Debbie said flatly. 'That's what you're trying to tell me isn't it? *You're* going to let her die.'

'She's alive but unconscious, Debbie. We're doing everything we can for her and I'd like you to help us.'

'Won't do any good,' Debbie said with a pout, twisting the frill of her nightie into a ball.

'Don't you want to help?'

Debbie's chin quivered as she went on twisting the frothy nylon, but she nodded as Alan continued: 'Your father has really made great strides during the past twenty-four hours, Debbie, but I don't want him upset, so you're on your honour to behave yourself if Sister Tyndall takes you along to see him. Then we'll see about taking you both up to see your mother.'

Debbie sniffed and wiped her eyes with her fingers.

'Are you sure Daddy wants to see me?'

'Of course, my dear, why wouldn't he?'

She took a sidelong glance at Claire and then buried her face in her hands. 'Because if Mummy dies he'll blame me. It was all my fault—he and I—we're always arguing. He says Mummy spoils me and he's very strict—oh—please—don't let her die, don't let Mummy die,' Debbie pleaded as tears of anguish poured down her cheeks.

Alan cuddled her to him for a few moments.

'You're going to help us to do everything we possibly can, Debbie,' he said comforting the distraught girl. 'Now I want you to get dressed and looking pretty for your father. What happened between you is over and forgotten, but he won't want to see a blotchy face and a pout.'

As Claire and Alan moved away Claire called a student nurse to go to help Debbie, and outside the ward Alan turned to Claire.

'At last Debbie's answered a few questions. This

behaviour pattern is a cover-up for guilt. I was beginning to think she would have to go to a psychiatric ward for investigation. Get her together with her father as soon as you can, Claire, and tomorrow, or by the weekend, let's hope we can get some response from Mrs Wilson. The Wilsons are top priority—your Mr Lynch can't expect to have you all to himself all the time.'

Claire was too stunned to reply as indignantly as she would have liked.

'I shall be in Miss Treadgold's domain tomorrow morning to see what progress is being made, I'll see if I can encourage Richard to persevere,' Alan added condescendingly.

He handed Claire the last folder, put his pen in his top pocket and with a nod left her looking after him with some impatience. She had been all ready and willing to compliment him on his handling of Debbie, but somehow he always aggravated her by making some personal quip about her and Richard. Long after he had left the unit and Claire had begun to supervise the serving of lunches, she was inwardly fuming at his implications, but after her own lunch she became too preoccupied with the Wilsons again to have time for personal grievances. She pushed Debbie in a wheelchair through the day room into the men's ward.

'Stay with me, Sister,' Debbie begged: 'Just for today—I don't know how I'm going to face him.'

'You're going to show him how much you love and care for him, Debbie—give him something to live for.'

But Debbie didn't need any such advice as father and daughter were reunited, and when Claire looked in on them before she went off duty for a couple of hours Mr Wilson had dropped off to sleep with Debbie's head cradled in the crook of his arm. She left instructions for Debbie to be taken back to bed within the hour, and Claire went to do her shopping. On the way out she stopped to look at the staff's notice board outside the canteen, and sure enough Mike had not only put her name on the fell-walk list but detailed her to provide some savoury refreshments.

In the supermarket car-park she had to drive round slowly looking for a vacant place, and when she saw a reversing light appear she pulled in indicating that she was going to take that place. As the car slowly emerged Claire saw that it was shiny and new, and the woman who was driving the sleek Granada raised her hand in acknowledgment to Claire before driving off. It was the same car and woman she had seen in the consultants' space at the hospital. Claire wished she had been able to get a closer view of the woman, but she experienced a momentary gnawing at her heart that one day it was inevitable that she should meet Alan Jarvis's wife.

She found herself wondering if they had children. Certainly the consultant had his own technique in handling teenage girls; and from there Claire's thoughts were back in the ward. With the Wilson family, Debbie in particular, and then Richard. She wished she could perform a miracle for him. The hardest part for him was yet to come. Children and young people were less self-conscious when it came to learning something, but for a man of nearly forty and of Richard's build, being able to walk was something you expected to do automatically. She half-expected to see him in the garden when she returned, but there was no sign of him until she reached the double doors, and then she had to wait for the porters to wheel a trolley through.

The voice of the disgruntled patient drew her attention immediately to the figure on the trolley and the nurse in attendance.

'Richard! What happened to you?' she asked anxiously.

'Nothing. I'm all right. I keep telling them, but they won't listen.'

Mike Boyd then appeared through the doorway. 'Richard had a fall, so we'll get him X-rayed just to be on the safe side.'

'I'm okay. It was nothing. I went down gently,' Richard explained.

'What were you doing?' Claire asked.

Richard didn't answer but the young nurse did. 'Trying to walk by himself.'

'I'll never get anywhere if I don't make myself do it,' Richard complained bitterly.

'One step at a time, I told you,' Claire reminded him firmly but with a note of compassion in her voice. 'I'll see you when you get back.'

The dark, gloomy expression lifted as Richard responded with raised eyebrows and Claire let the trolley pass.

Claire had no time though to give Richard any special treatment. Later when he was returned to the ward the report was that he had done no further damage as far as they could tell, and the nurse and porters helped him back to bed.

Sister Cannon was off duty so Claire had to be on hand for that ward as well as her own and the time slipped by until at quarter to ten Mim looked in.

'Late turn?' she asked coming to stand by Claire's desk.

'Yes, and the whole weekend working.'

'It all seems fairly quiet. I've just done my round of your patients, everyone is settled. I hear Mr Lynch had a fall?'

'Yes, I was off duty so I don't really know exactly what happened, but I gather he was trying to walk by himself.'

'He'll be too nervous to try that again. Thank goodness he didn't do any damage! Debbie Wilson is fast asleep, which makes a nice change. She's usually demanding to see late night television at this hour.'

Claire briefly related what had taken place earlier in the day, then she completed her report and handed over to Miriam.

The following day the condition of Mrs Wilson caused the medical team to step up Debbie's visit to her mother. Alan came himself and escorted Debbie up to the I.T.U., and after they had gone Claire reflected sadly over his report of the case.

'She's deteriorating slightly, I'm afraid, Claire,' he had explained. 'Perhaps Debbie is the missing link. I don't feel Mr Wilson is quite well enough today, but at least he and Debbie are on good terms now.'

When Debbie was brought back to Ward Two she was subdued, and later asked that she could sit with her father, which she was allowed to do, but at the end of the day Mrs Wilson was still in the same critical condition. It cast a shadow of despondency over everyone, the staff in particular low-spirited with an impending doom of failure in their minds.

Through Mr Wilson and Debbie, Claire felt closely connected with Mrs Wilson, and she spent a few moments herself talking to the unconscious woman, explaining that Debbie and her husband were well on the way to a full recovery, that they spent some time happily together. She went home feeling frustrated that there was no response. Could Mrs Wilson hear? Had she shut herself off from the world to avoid knowing the fate of her husband and daughter? Was she somewhere suspended in a limbo of dread of the relationship between Mr Wilson and Debbie? No one would ever know. They could only persevere, and the next day being Sunday it was the hospital chaplain who joined in the effort to draw Mrs Wilson back to consciousness.

Later on in the day, after lunch when visitors had arrived in vast numbers, Claire was surprised to hear Alan Jarvis approaching. He had a distinctive walk as he came through the corridor. She was busy at her desk catching up on the volume of paperwork which had accrued when he entered her office briskly.

'Claire—if the Wilsons get any visitors, can you send them off somewhere to get a cup of tea? I've detailed the porters to take Debbie and Mr Wilson up to I.T.U.'

'The Wilsons come from down south, so I doubt that there will be any visitors today,' Claire said.

'Good—I'm hoping they'll be willing to stay for several hours, reacting as they would if they were ordinary visitors.'

'Mr Wilson is quite remarkable.'

'He's determined to live for Debbie's sake. Bringing him from I.T.U. was the right thing for both of them. They've got each other and can put up a united front to bring Mrs Wilson round. I know you've got plenty on down here, so don't worry about them, leave the Wilsons to me.'

He gave her a flashing smile and was gone. Claire stared into space, awe-inspired by Alan Jarvis, a consultant surgeon who cared enough about his patients to give up his time on a Sunday. The one day of the week when everything was usually left for the registrar and housemen to deal with. The one day of the week which consultants expected to share with their wives and families.

Strange that Alan Jarvis should neglect his attractive wife. He had been in and out of the hospital yesterday, and now again today. Claire wondered just how far his personal involvement was allowed to progress, and what type of woman was the glamorous driver of the Granada to take second place in his life?

Tea-time on Sundays were pleasant, light-hearted affairs. Some patients were allowed to go for a short drive with their families, encouraged to do so during the lovely fine spell of weather, while others enjoyed the freedom and beauty of the gardens at Moorlands Hospital. Auxiliary nurses pushed the tea-trolleys out on to a large cemented patio where the visitors could come to collect tea-trays often supplying home-prepared delicacies themselves and usually bringing far more than was necessary so that the nursing staff benefitted from their generosity.

Claire went outside to mingle and chat with the wives and members of patients' families who had quickly become friends. She laughed when she saw huge bowls of trifles, fruit, jelly and ice-cream which was being shared out, and she remembered Richard who had no one to bring him extra goodies. It was as if Mr Whitmarsh's daughter, a girl of about Claire's own age, had read Claire's thoughts when she asked if there was anyone who had no company. Claire explained about Richard.

'I'd better go and ask him first,' she said, and went through open french windows into the day rooms which were at the end of each ward.

The doors were all closed, the curtains drawn in the small day room where Richard could usually be found.

Claire gasped in disbelief at the empty wheelchair in the corner.

Surely Richard couldn't be resting now?

She heard a grunt, and from the shadow of a curtain in an alcove, a figure tottered precariously—one—step—then another—and the next one—surely he must fall—and Claire rushed forward to catch Richard.

But as they clung together it felt to Claire that Richard was holding her up.

'Richard—that was wonderful,' Claire breathed, so overwhelmed that she couldn't hide the tears of joy which ran down her cheeks.

She looked up into Richard's face, aglow with self-satisfaction, and then without any premeditation their lips came together, deliciously, fiercely, sealing the emotion which Claire had tried to keep under control. Richard held her firm in his embrace as his smooth, demanding mouth sought to claim hers again and again.

CHAPTER FIVE

EVENTUALLY Claire broke free and laughed. 'I came to ask if you'd like some trifle for tea,' she said with a chuckle.

'What I've just experienced, darling, is worth more than all the jelly and trifle in the world,' Richard whispered.

'That was only my reward for your first steps,' she teased, her face alight with admiration.

Richard smiled lovingly down into her upturned face.

'So what do I get when I take a dozen or more?' he asked.

'Wait and see,' she answered, making a face at him. 'Don't get greedy.'

'I was only working towards a dinner date, now the prospects seem endless.' He looked so pleased with himself that Claire was carried along with his enthusiasm.

'Richard, you really have done wonderfully well. I'm proud of you. Can you do it again? Just for me—I can hardly believe it,' Claire urged excitedly.

She stood back still holding his hand until she was sure he was balanced properly, then she gently pulled her fingers away and slid her feet back a few paces.

Richard kept his gaze directed at her and for what seemed like ages he didn't move, then he repeated his earlier success.

One—two—three—and at the fourth step, as he reached Claire and held her fast, a clap from the curtained doorway made them both start.

'I agree with Sister Tyndall, Mr Lynch, you have persevered excellently—well done.'

Alan Jarvis walked forward to shake Richard's hand and pat him on the shoulder, but his face did not reflect the joy which both Richard and Claire were demonstrating. Claire looked round for a chair, Richard's chair, anything so long as she could sever the contact for which Alan Jarvis was silently condemning her.

'Perhaps you'd like to go out into the garden for tea?' she suggested brightly, her cheeks stained with deep crimson guilt.

'A splendid idea, Mr Lynch, but I suspect that measure of excitement is enough for one day. We don't want you falling again, so I suggest you rely on the chair until you gain more confidence.'

'I wanted to surprise Cl . . . Sister Tyndall, and I succeeded, now my next aim is a weekend out of this place,' Richard said eagerly.

'But you've no home in this country, Mr Lynch,' Alan reminded him.

'No matter, Mr Jarvis,' Richard said confidently. 'There are plenty of hotels, and taxis which will take me to some beauty spot for a change.'

'I admire your courage, Mr Lynch,' Alan said, but there was a sharpness in his manner. 'Sister, may I beg a cup of tea before I leave?—perhaps you can find someone else to take care of Mr Lynch.'

Claire had pulled Richard's chair up to him. She helped him into it not daring to look at either man as her cheeks were all too depictive of the embarrassment she was feeling.

She went thankfully out into the sunshine where the sweet fresh air fanned her cheeks cool again, and she called one of the nurses to come and see that Richard had some tea.

When she reached her office with a tea-tray for herself and the consultant she felt calmer and almost ready for the reproach she expected. Alan Jarvis was sprawled casually in the easy chair, his long legs seeming to span the length of the small office.

Claire was trying to collect her thoughts together. How much had he seen? At what point had he crept unheeded up to the small alcove door? It was a despicable thing to do, creeping about, trying to catch her out. And that was the trouble. She had given him cause to do it again whenever he chose! What madness had possessed them? Of course, Richard could walk; it was cause enough to celebrate. But hardly in the way that they had chosen.

'You must feel quite elated, Sister—Claire,' Alan said. 'To see a patient walking again, just those first few steps is most encouraging to patient and nurse alike.'

'Not to you?' she asked quickly.

'But of course, though you girls have so much more to do with the patients than us doctors.'

'It's job satisfaction for all of us,' Claire said decidedly. She handed Alan a cup of tea and knew that his subtle dark eyes were assessing her agitation. She managed to hold the plate steady as she offered him a small iced cake.

'Mm—cake on Sundays?' he perceived.

'The patients look forward to something from home, and lots of the relatives show their appreciation to the staff this way. By the volume of goodies I've seen today we shall be well stocked for the rest of the week.'

'It's very sweet of you to include me, Claire, but I do feel such gifts are intended for the more junior nurses.'

'I've had several boxes of chocolates, a gâteau, a chocolate roll, a sponge, and two cheesecakes as well as a box full of these fancy cakes all left in my office, and a similar amount has also been given to the nursing staff for the patients, probably more. The general public imagine that we eat only bread and water in hospitals.'

'We enjoy a lot more variety than that, don't we, Claire?'

Claire glanced briefly towards Alan, knowing by the

derisive tone of his voice that he was mocking her confusion, but as he emptied his mouth he added: 'Quite delicious, though, and I'm not above being spoilt on Sundays.' He paused to sip his tea. 'I hope Mr Lynch doesn't expect to be as spoilt after each attempt to walk as he was today?'

Claire felt the blood surging from her neck upwards.

'After all,' Alan added, 'he'll go on improving, a kiss a step—what will it lead to? Where will it end?'

Claire refused to look at him. Only she and Richard could know the passion that had been in those kisses.

'I suppose you're going to tell me that you got carried away?' Alan persisted. Why couldn't he drop it? she thought.

At last she managed to find her voice, however humble it sounded. 'I'm not going to tell you anything, Mr Jarvis, nor will I bother to make excuses.'

He stood up and placed the cup and saucer on the tray on the desk, and inwardly Claire breathed a sigh of relief. He was going—perhaps the intimate scene which she now knew he had witnessed had reminded him that he had a wife at home waiting for him.

But Alan Jarvis had not done with her yet. He stood over her, his hand first on her shoulder then as his face drew near to hers she felt his hand moulding her shoulder blade, down and round to the front of her, fingers creeping under the bib of her white apron. At the same time his lips nibbled at her ear. This was too much of a liberty, and Claire turned her head sharply to remonstrate, but his lips were quick to take advantage of the close proximity, and she found herself powerless in his magnetic hold, his mouth demanding—all too demanding—on hers.

When he broke away his hand was encasing her neck, and the delightful feel of his smooth fingers caressing her bare skin sent ice-cold shivers down her spine even though her body was aflame. He smiled down at her puzzled expression with eyes full of bedevilled wickedness.

'I told you, Claire, I'm not above being spoilt on Sundays.' He gave her neck a playful squeeze and then stood up straight with a slight groan of impatience. 'Sorry I have to rush away, but Fiona has me earmarked for some dreadful theatre party. Such a depressing thought—that Sundays don't last for ever, I mean.'

He sort of swung on his heel as if he would have preferred to stay, but duty was calling him away. There was a boyish lightness about the way he walked to the door and stood swinging it on its hinges as he carefully chose his parting words.

'You're on duty for a few more hours?' he asked.

'Until eight.' By now Claire was recovering, and she stood up to face him as he closed the door and stood with his back to it.

'Be careful, Claire—I would advise against too much excitement for Mr Lynch, even though it is Sunday. Remember the ruling about involvement.'

Maybe the sudden ardour of the consultant had momentarily undermined Claire's spirit, but with a hasty upsurge of anger, her eyes burning with petulance, she answered: 'Doesn't it apply to us all?'

His face seemed to darken as he stepped forward again towards her.

'Meaning?' he demanded.

'We don't usually see consultants much at weekends.'

'In our profession, my dear, none of us are ever one hundred per cent off duty. But there is a difference in taking an interest in a patient's progress and rewarding one in such an intimate way—however elated you may both have felt.'

'I didn't plan it,' Claire answered hotly. 'Naturally I was thrilled for Richard, and I automatically tried to prevent him from falling—the rest—just—happened.'

Alan advanced to meet her until there was barely a

space between them.

'And it will be difficult to refrain from allowing it to happen again—won't it, Claire?' he asked softly.

Why did he gaze into her face so benignly? Why did his eyes glow with warmth? and the mellowness in them reduce her to complaisant submission?

'Just a Sunday treat—eh?' His hands were on her elbows drawing her to bridge the gap and she weakened even more at the throb of desire she felt at his nearness. 'As long as you treat us all alike,' he added, and before she could move backwards as she knew she ought, he was clasping her to him, his sensual mouth drawing every ounce of passion from between her lips as he effortlessly parted them with his tongue. His slender fingers moved over her back at the same time, sliding round her slim waist, moulding her hips, reminding her of the alluring attraction a feminine body holds for a man.

She had placed her hands against his chest at the first impact, now they were trapped, and she was helpless in his embrace. When he released her gently he took both her hands in his and kept them pressed against his torso. His gaze consumed hers so that they didn't speak. Mellowness was still there but with a flame of desire added, and the hardness of his muscles against her body made every pulse in Claire's react violently.

Wild thoughts ran through her mind. Alan Jarvis was incredibly handsome, but beneath the suave sophistication he was a wolf, ready to devour any female who would fall victim to his attentions.

She felt him stiffen and move back a pace.

'Claire,' he said gently, 'you surely don't think I'd fall for Debbie Wilson's teenage nymphomania?'

Claire couldn't answer. She was forced to lower her gaze to the middle button of his jacket. Wasn't that just what had niggled at the back of her mind? And he already a married man!

'Claire!' Alan admonished severely. 'She's only a child. Throwing her clothes around does not stir my emotions—only a woman can do that.'

His mouth, forceful and hard against her lips, was savage in the extreme, the attack so unexpected that Claire was forced to cry out with pain. Alan was merciless and when he did let her go he almost flung her away from him.

'A *woman*, Claire,' he reminded her, and abruptly stalked off, slamming the door behind him.

Claire quickly sat down at her desk, pressing her clammy fingers to her temples. Inside she felt shivery, the outward calm a façade. Of course it was ridiculous to think of any consultant reacting to a teenage girl's provocation. Hadn't he treated Debbie as a father would do? Claire had even given him credit for the way he handled her, and yet she was aware of an unusual interest shown by him for Debbie. It was only because of the critical condition of both her parents, her subconscious reiterated yet again.

She pressed her fingers to her lips, which burned with the sensual persuasiveness of Alan's. Her eyes flickered over the pages of the report book as if to remind her that only moments before it had been Richard Lynch whose kisses had urged a response. That, she mused wryly, had been a mutual response. A deep attraction, along with a sense of caring for a man who seemed to have no one else in the world had brought about such a unison.

Claire found herself idly toying with her pen. Both men were married. What sort of girl must she be to attract that sort? It made her feel cheap, caused her heart to ache with the knowledge that however confused about Richard or Alan she felt, neither one of them was eligible.

At least Richard had been honest in so much as that he admitted he had a wife—'there was once, there isn't now'. Separated? divorced?—even a widower perhaps?

Claire shrugged that thought away. His attitudes were not those of a bereaved man. He was bitter, fretful, but for what reason? She had taken it for granted that it was because of his condition, but in her heart she suspected that there were other reasons for his unsociability. She had won him round, though. He showed pleasure at her caring, even if she still had learned nothing of importance about him.

Alan Jarvis had shown pleasure in taunting her. He had held her close, kissed her, caressed her with what she had interpreted as affection, yet now she realised that there must be other motives. Claire stared down blankly at the neatly-written pages of the report book in front of her. She didn't want to compare the two men, but if it came to choosing—she sighed, saddened by the knowledge that Alan Jarvis had aroused something in her which no man had done before.

He was a consultant, he had a very glamorous wife— something to do with the theatre, he had said. Claire decided that if that were the case it excused his lack of decent moral behaviour. Perhaps his wife made a habit of flirting with other men, even having more serious relationships, and consultants were not above having a bit on the side, a diversion.

The trouble was, Claire reflected, it was usually the woman in such cases who got hurt. She had no intention of allowing him to make use of her. He had insinuated that if it hadn't been for this theatre party he would have—she felt the blood coursing through her veins at what might have been.

She was glad of the opportunity of remaining in her office to make the relevant notes about each patient, also thankful that, for a while at least, most of them were being cared for by members of their own families. She tried to push away troublesome personal thoughts but they kept intruding, no matter how hard she tried to concentrate on her report. The minutes were ticking by towards the end of visiting time, and her aim was to complete the paperwork before any interruptions, but the telephone bell jangled obtrusively. She picked up the receiver.

'Sister Tyndall speaking,' she said calmly.

'Claire—Alan Jarvis here.' The smooth masculine voice caused her heart to flip, and there was a pause before he continued: 'In the recent excitement I forgot to mention that I shall leave it to you and Sister Burgess to arrange the comings and goings of Mr Wilson and Debbie. If the visits to I.T.U. appear to upset them in any way, keep it in low profile.'

'Yes, of course.' Her voice sounded much more steady than her heart was beating. She waited, loving the lilt of his voice in her ear, breathlessly wanting the conversation to go on.

'Oh, and Claire——'

'Yes?'

'Has anyone ever told you what a deep, sexy voice you have on the telephone?'

'No,' she answered, trying to keep the tremor from it and wishing he hadn't made such a comment.

'Well you have, and you'd better be careful who you purr to.'

'I don't intentionally purr to anyone,' she replied shortly, irritated that he had spoilt the conversation by insinuating that she set out to attract attention. She heard a low, throaty chuckle.

'That's part of a woman's charm, Claire, to purr at the right time, with the spitting and clawing to add intrigue and arouse a man's passion.'

Claire decided that the conversation was becoming too personal and then in the background she heard a high-pitched voice calling to Alan to hurry up.

'I'm wanted,' he said curtly. 'I'd better go or the spitting will be a reality and aimed at me. Look after Debbie for me, Claire.'

She heard the click as the telephone was replaced at his end, and she sat for a couple of seconds listening to the burr in her ear.

He was only flirting with her. She let the receiver drop on to its rest with a hollow clatter as she felt her nerves tighten with annoyance. She didn't need to ponder for long before coming to the conclusion that the reason for this flirtation was obvious. He had witnessed the intimate scene between herself and Richard, and he had taken it upon himself to break up the relationship. He was married, tied down to a woman who clearly dominated him, by the tone of the distant voice, so he was a spoilsport, a killjoy when he glimpsed someone else's happiness.

Happiness. Claire mulled the word over in her mind. It took so little to make a woman happy she reflected. The right word, a smile, a touch—yes, it was a touch that mattered most. However light and unintentional, a brush of a man's skin against her own—— At the mere reminder of Alan's skilful hands moving over her body she felt again the tingle of desire, and she rebuked herself for indulging in any desirous thoughts for Alan Jarvis.

Her reverie was cut off sharply as the bell peeled outside in the corridor, announcing that visitors must leave. Claire straightened her cap, smoothed her apron and went out into the corridor. They came in twos and threes into the corridor, but all wanting to stop and chat to Claire, anxious that the patient remaining in her care had every comfort as well as hoping to hear whether discharge was imminent. Getting to know the relatives was as important as understanding the patient, Claire realised.

Gradually the wards reverted to the quiet place of healing. The young nurses rounded up the more active patients and Claire did her final round of the day, surprised to find Debbie in bed and huddled beneath the sheets.

'She wants to be left alone,' Tricia Cannon explained in a hushed voice.

Claire placed a gentle hand on Debbie's shoulder.

'Are you all right, Debbie?'

The tousled fair head nodded, but she kept her face hidden, so Claire whispered, 'Goodnight, God bless,' and moved on.

When Claire reached Mr Wilson he too was lying still with his eyes closed.

'Anything I can get you, Mr Wilson?' Claire asked.

He shook his head but opened his eyes.

'Nothing I want, Sister, only for Maggie to come back to us.'

'Has it tired you, Mr Wilson?'

He sighed despondently. 'A bit, but it seemed such useless effort and Debbie's so young, she finds it hard to understand and is quick to lose faith.'

'We must keep persevering, Mr Wilson, but don't go if it tires you too much or upsets Debbie.'

'She says she doesn't want to go again, but by tomorrow she'll have changed her mind. I must go—every day.'

'There was no response, then?' Claire asked.

'None—but the Sister up there says she's no worse—physically, that is.'

'Just a short visit each day until you feel stronger,' Claire advised, and she still felt sad as she went on to find Richard.

He was sitting in his usual place but reading. He glanced up when he heard her footsteps.

'You've taken your time,' he greeted, with a sparkle in his dark eyes.

'I'm due to go off now. You don't feel tired after your great achievement today?'

Richard laughed outright. 'Some achievement, three or four steps!'

'It *was* an achievement, Richard. Learning to walk again is no easy thing but gradually now each day will help you to get stronger and more confident.'

'I expect you're right, and it will be worth it to get my reward.'

Claire looked at him with a puzzled frown.

'Oh, I must admit the reward I had today was delightful and unexpected. My goal is that weekend with you,' he said forcibly.

'I thought it was a dinner date.'

'But I owe you so much, darling. I'd like to have you all to myself away from the hospital. No strings, Claire—just let me give you a good time to thank you properly.'

'Once you're dashing around, Richard, you won't give me a second thought. You'll be off and anxious to get back into business.'

'Don't say things like that, darling. It almost sounds as if you have cause for such bitterness, and I'm sure you can't have. Any eligible fellow would be insane to let you slip through his fingers. I suppose most of them, though, don't bother to find out what's beneath the starch and bedside manner.'

'Shouldn't the bedside manner be sufficient?'

His ebony depths flickered over her in no mean manner.

'After the bedside manner comes the "in-bed" perfomance—that's the test.'

Claire tossed her head, her cheeks pink.

'See what I mean?' Richard continued. 'Just look in the mirror and you'll see the pure, innocent, dedicated nursing sister. You were made for a man to love, Claire.'

'And you're being dangerously familiar, Mr Lynch.'

Richard smiled. 'Don't go all pious on me. Did you get a rocket for being too familiar with a patient?' he asked with a grin.

'No—just a facetious reminder that you'd had enough excitement for one day, and that I can spoil you on Sundays.'

'Big deal!' Richard laughed, and Claire thought how pleasant it was to hear the sound of merriment coming from him. He had reached a milestone today, and she was glad that she had been there to witness it and share the joy with him, no matter what Alan Jarvis thought. But Alan Jarvis had given her something to think about too, for Claire was mildly conscious of the fact that his kisses had aroused a deeper, inner feeling, a feeling of desperate longing, whereas Richard's passion had been a momentary surface experience. She wanted to encounter the former event a second time. Had it really happened or was it her imagination playing tricks? Was it just flattery that was causing her to want Alan to illustrate his prowess again?

Much later that evening after she had reached her flat, eaten, and done a few necessary tasks, she submitted to weariness and an awareness of emotional confusion, but after a good night's sleep she returned to the hospital content to put her patients before all else. She loved the hurry and urgency of a Monday morning, never knowing just what the beginning of a working week would bring forth, and she had the added stimulant of a weekend off to look forward to.

When she heard the shuffle of feet as the swing doors were pushed open Claire was suddenly seized with panic at the prospect of having to face Alan Jarvis after what had taken place the previous day. Did the feeling of impending excitement show in her face? She tried to stay the bubbling frenzy which threatened to erupt. A mixture of nerves, guilt, and expectancy.

It was Mike Boyd who came to find her.

'Hi, Claire.' He looked serious and bent to speak low

into her ear. 'Can we get into the ward? His Lordship is in the most foul mood.'

'Who's upset him?' Claire asked with a smile.

'Goodness knows—he came in with a roar.'

Claire needn't have worried about meeting Alan. He nodded a curt greeting in her direction as she joined him at the first patient's bed in Ward One, and after speaking briefly to each one he moved swiftly on until they had finished, then with a dark impatient frown he asked: 'Any problems?'

'No, I don't think so,' she began.

'I haven't time to wait while you think, Sister. I shall be away for most of the week, so Dr Boyd will be in charge. Keep the Wilsons as top priority—watch Debbie's breathing, and encourage her with her breathing exercises.' He nodded again in curt dismissal and walked off briskly through the corridor.

Mike managed to give Claire a playful or meaningful pinch as he passed by, and the retinue of doctors followed the consultant, leaving Claire bemused. He was in too much of a hurry even to stop for coffee, or was he planning to enjoy that in another department?

Claire went to see Debbie after the physiotherapist had left her ward. She seemed to have become morose, hardly speaking to anyone except her father since yesterday.

'What do you feel like doing today, Debbie? Going to see your father?' Claire suggested kindly.

Debbie nodded. She was pale, almost waxlike and the green of her eyes appeared to have faded over the last few days. Claire helped her to stand and together they went slowly out to the day room.

'It's still beautiful, and so warm perhaps you'd like to sit outside for a while?' Claire said.

'Daddy will want to go and sit with Mummy, but what's the use? She's never going to come round is she?'

'We don't know, Debbie, but if talking to her helps

then it's worth it, surely?'

'But you feel so stupid, talking to someone who doesn't answer, and anyway what can we talk about?'

Mr Wilson was already sitting in a wheelchair. Both legs had been injured, one foot so severely crushed that amputation had been necessary. He seemed like the Invisible Man, swathed in bandages.

'I wondered if you'd like to sit in the sunshine for a while, Mr Wilson?'

He smiled at Claire and she thought how pathetic he looked.

'Hullo, darling,' he greeted Debbie. 'What would you like to do?'

'I expect you'd prefer to go and sit with Mummy, but is it any good?—I mean, I just can't think of anything to say.'

'I know how you feel, darling, but we must try,' he pleaded.

'Just talking to each other might help,' Claire said. 'Talk about past holidays, happy memories, visiting relatives or friends. Plan what you're going to do in the future, exciting things which will include Mrs Wilson—just talk as if you were around your own fireside, or dining table. Forget about the accident and your injuries—be happy together as a family—it's worth a try,' Claire suggested thoughtfully.

'I suppose so,' Debbie agreed reluctantly. 'We can come back for lunch, can't we? Then we can go outside for a while?'

'Of course—make the most of the sunshine while it's here. It can't possibly last longer than a fortnight,' Claire said with a laugh.

She pushed Mr Wilson herself, with Debbie holding on to the chair, to the lift and up to I.T.U. where Mrs Wilson still remained motionless, and somewhere far away in a land unknown to anyone else. Claire leaned over the patient.

'Good morning, Mrs Wilson,' she said in a soft but cheery voice. 'I've brought your husband along to see you, and Debbie too. They're really doing fine—but they'll tell you all the news themselves.'

Not even the flutter of an eyelid was the response, and as Claire wheeled Mr Wilson closer to the bedside she felt an empty void, a sense of failure, an understanding of the anguish both Mr Wilson and Debbie were feeling.

She left them quickly, knowing that they were experiencing a certain self-consciousness, and as each day passed they returned to Claire's unit looking unhappy and dejected. But for every failure there was one success, often more, and Claire shared Richard's jubilation when towards the weekend he was able to walk with the aid of his two sticks as far as the car-park.

'Next weekend it will be only one stick, and the following one you'll walk me to the car-park unaided,' Claire told him.

'Then I shall really feel I'm making progress. You're due for some time off by now, surely?' Richard asked.

'The weekend, from Saturday lunch time round until Monday lunch time.'

'I shall miss you.'

'You wouldn't if you tried to join in with the others.'

'I know you mean well, but I can't suddenly start intruding into their little groups, can I?'

'Of course you can. Offer someone one of your paperbacks, that's always a good way to open a conversation. And anyway, several have gone home over the last couple of days, so there are some new people you can chat up—Mr Wilson and Debbie. Now they do need someone different to talk to, especially when they come back from I.T.U.'

'Still no response from Mrs Wilson?'

Claire shook her head. 'If only there was something

else we could try!'

'You're too good for all of us, Claire darling. The N.H.S. and the medical profession takes a hammering, but I have a lot to thank you all for—you especially.'

'I've done nothing,' she said, 'nothing that I wouldn't have done for anyone else.'

'You've done everything, and I don't begrudge you your weekend off, but how are you going to spend it?'

'If the weather remains good we're going walking.'

'We?' Richard's eyebrows shot up in anticipation.

'Some of the staff. Not my idea—Mike's the organiser. He feels it's necessary as we aren't situated too close to a large town with all its facilities. We have to make our own recreational pleasures.'

'That shouldn't be too difficult—where there are both sexes involved.'

'Not a lot of variety, though, when you all meet through work anyway.'

'But you see a different side when you're away from the hospital. I'm looking forward to seeing Claire, the woman.'

'Meaning that when I'm on duty I'm some sort of freak—a robot, perhaps?'

'I don't care what you are, as long as you make all the right movements when the time comes.'

'You've got a one-track mind like most men,' she admonished light-heartedly.

'If you're out and about over the weekend, Claire, pick us a nice spot to spend our weekend. Choose a cosy hotel.'

'I . . . I've only agreed to a dinner date,' she said guardedly.

'All right. Pick *me* a nice hotel so that I can invite you there to dinner.'

'There's plenty of time, and plenty of literature in the hospital library.'

'I mean it, Claire.' Richard put the stick from his right

hand into the left one and encircled Claire in his right arm. He squeezed her gently and pulled her round to face him. There was something very sensual about him, and she found it easy to respond to his charm. She kissed him back because she wanted to kiss him, wanted to experience the warmth of feeling, the passion however brief which made her aware of herself as a woman. He made her feel needed as a woman, not just as a nurse. But she pulled away, always conscious that someone might see them though they were in the shrubbery, hidden from view by colourful azaleas and tall rhododendrons.

'Kiss me again, Claire—and again,' he pleaded between each, 'the weekend is going to seem endless.'

Their lips met and remained sealed, charged with impetuosity, and Claire cursed Mike Boyd for involving her in the weekend's activities, which allowed her no room or time to take Richard out for a drive: a thought which was uppermost in her mind, and had been ever since he had suggested the dinner date. She knew she was allowing herself to become dangerously entangled with a patient, but at twenty-five years old wasn't it time she lived dangerously?

CHAPTER SIX

WHEN Claire was due to leave the hospital at midday on Saturday, the sun had only just appeared. There had been an early morning mist which had taken considerably longer to clear than usual, so that the day rooms had been well used during the morning.

Mr Wilson and Debbie had occupied the room Richard normally used, while he was at a physiotherapy class, and when Claire went to say goodbye to Richard she found him in earnest conversation with them. He suggested walking across the garden with her, and Debbie offered to accompany him. Richard hid his disappointment well, and before they reached the shrubbery suggested turning back.

'Don't forget to find somewhere for me to stay, Sister,' Richard added as Claire gave a final wave. She acknowledged his request with a smile, and walked on through the shrubbery thinking how casual he had been.

He was an unpredictable man. Just when she expected him to show irritation he appeared his most charming, and although she felt a little downcast that there had been no opportunity of a few minutes alone together, she was pleased that he had entered into companionship with the Wilsons. Now she could go home and really relax for the weekend, knowing that Richard wouldn't be lonely, and that the Wilsons would have someone else to mix with when they were not in the Intensive Care Unit.

But of course, she reflected drily, relaxation was out of the question; she'd been detailed to go on the fell-walk, and to supply a quantity of food. That meant that she would have to spend the afternoon baking, so on her way home she stopped off at the supermarket to buy cheese, tomatoes, spring onions, and a tin of salmon with which to make the filling for the *vol-au-vents*.

On reaching her flat she put the car away in the garage and walked through the narrow pathway which led to a small gate at the bottom of the garden. As always she took off her shoes when she got indoors then padded in her stockinged feet to the small porch at the front where she found she had some mail. For once no bills, she sighed thankfully, and mentally noted that one letter was from her friend still nursing in the hospital in York, one from her father in London and the third was a larger-sized buff envelope which on further scrutiny she discovered had been posted in Wiltshire.

The next part of the usual ritual was to remove her uniform, put the kettle on, and prepare a meal if she hadn't eaten at the hospital. She did hastily slip out of most of her clothes and switched the kettle on, and while she waited she tore open the buff envelope. It contained a full star reading as promised from Karlotta, but after reading the first few lines which indicated where the major planets were at the time of her birth, she tossed it to one side as being unimportant.

While the cauliflower was cooking for her favourite dish of cauliflower au gratin she made tea in her tiny teapot and carried it into the lounge, where she curled up on the settee to read her letters. She chose the one from her friend to read first: Sandy was an abbreviation of Sandra as well as being an apt description of her friend's hair, which waved in lustrous scrolls framing her round face, which also nearly matched the colour of her hair with an abundance of freckles.

Sandy's letter was full of hospital gossip, colourful as well as descriptive of her social and working life, and inviting Claire to get down to York for a weekend or longer during the summer if she could. Claire usually returned to York each year, not only to see her friends from the hospital but to delight in her favourite haunts and to discover places she had as yet not explored in the vast city, so historic and still alive with the ancient past.

Claire sighed nostalgically as she replaced Sandy's letter in the envelope, and opened the one from her father. He too was anxious that Claire should visit London, and she felt as she always did after reading his letters, a little sad. Sad that so many miles separated them, sad that his home did not include her as one of the key members of his household. Claire realised that it was not her father's fault; neither was he aware of her feeling the way she did. She had always got on well with her stepmother, but with a family of three of their own Claire had sensed that she was an outsider. Which was why, after qualifying in a London hospital, she had chosen to accept the post in York.

Claire sipped her tea as she re-read her father's letter and felt guilty at the hidden reproach that she had preferred to go to Spain for her holiday rather than going to visit him and his family. She uncurled her shapely legs; soon she must organise those trips and the remaining holiday due to her, but the memory of Spain jolted her to pick up the third letter. Karlotta and her star-gazing! On holiday she had been known as Charlotte Tarrazona and she claimed to be part Italian. Claire could look back on her holiday now with amusement. She supposed she had hoped to find some dishy, unattached bachelor with whom she could have enjoyed a mild relationship, instead she had been shadowed constantly by Charlotte, alias Karlotta, world-famous astrologer.

Claire returned to the kitchen, prepared her cheese sauce and sat down at her small formica-topped table to enjoy her meal, with the closely typewritten astrological reading propped up against the cruet.

Gradually she found herself becoming absorbed by what she read, most of it surprisingly accurate regarding her character and emotions. She had a strong desire to meet the right man who would make her happy in marriage, Karlotta wrote. Being a Piscean she wore her heart on her sleeve and did not always react the way men expected. She was emotional, sensitive, but also quick and fiery-tempered on occasion. Karlotta then went on to predict that her future path would not carry her along on the same professional route. There would be changes according to which of the three men who dominated her life she chose to be her partner, and this was likely to be the man who seemed the least eligible.

Claire's thoughts turned eagerly to Richard. He seemed the least eligible, she decided, because of his detachment from the outside world, and let's face it, she mused ironically, he was the only suitable man she knew. It was true there was Mike, but he was a stalwart friend, nothing more, and although her thoughts wafted towards Alan Jarvis from time to time, being a married man and consultant he didn't even count.

Her spirits lifted a little at the mere hint of a third man coming into her life so that she skipped through the rest of her life-guide as she finished eating, and then she put it away. Karlotta advised her to read it several times during the coming weeks and a short letter repeated the invitation to Wiltshire. Claire smiled, wondering if Karlotta, or Charlotte as she thought of her, was weaving her own plan of future events including this brother of hers as a suitor for Claire. Although Claire had no notion of his age or type, she was convinced that he wouldn't rate in her list of eligible men.

She put on her overall and spent the rest of the afternoon baking, which she enjoyed doing, and when the pastries were all arranged on her long working surface Claire felt pride and satisfaction in her afternoon's labour. While they were cooling she decided to go and sit in the garden but she had only been there for about half an hour when it became cloudy and dull. Hadn't she said it couldn't last for ever? The weather had been so warm and sunny through the first half of May that it was bound to change for her weekend off. She went inside, showered, and put on a crimplene dress, then packed the food she had prepared in cling-film wrapping before placing it in airtight storage boxes.

She wondered how many people would finally set out on the walk the next day, and hoped Mike didn't expect her and Mim to carry all the food. She really could have done with a Sunday just to herself, but, she reflected, she supposed she would soon get bored with her own company. She sorted out her jeans, tee-shirt, sweater, thick socks and sturdy brogue shoes ready for the morning, then settled down to watch a variety programme on television before the evening film.

She prepared a light meal on a tray and before she had even reached the lounge with it the doorbell rang. She quickly took the tray to the low glass-topped coffee table in the lounge when the doorbell rang again, impatiently.

Claire was surprised to find Miriam on the doorstep.

'Oh, thank goodness you're there, Claire,' she said pushing a polythene carrier bag into Claire's arms.

'You might give me time to get to the door,' Claire said goodnaturedly.

'Thought you might have gone out—or been in bed—or—you know?' Miriam raised her eyebrows suggestively.

Claire laughed. 'No such luck, and I am alone so you can come in,' she invited.

'Wish I could, love, but you'll never guess—Sylvia Cresswell has gone sick, so bang go my nights off.'

'Oh, Mim, that's tough luck,' Claire sympathised.

'You can say that again—not that I wanted to go hiking all over the Yorkshire dales, but the fresh air would have been good for me, and it would have been a change from hiking all over Moorlands wards and corridors.'

'You might be grateful for the change of plan,' Claire said glancing up at the darkening sky. 'Looks to me as if we're in for a storm.'

'According to the weather forecast there might be a little light rain overnight, followed by mist in the morning with the good weather continuing,' Mim said. 'I made a point of listening to the forecast—before I received the phone call—so I thought I'd better drop my edible contribution in to you. I prepared the sandwiches three or four days ago and they've been in our freezer, so if you can find room in your fridge till the morning I'd be very grateful.'

'Sure—who else is supplying food?' Claire asked.

'Mike said he'd bring fruit and drinks—I bet he hasn't had the cheek to detail anyone else into bringing anything.'

'We always get lumbered—next time he can find someone else,' Claire grumbled.

'He knows he can rely on you to come up with those delicious pastries. Can't think why he doesn't marry you—if only for your cooking,' Mim said with a grin.

'Mike sees me as the sensible, steady type—not marriageable in his eyes.'

'Hmph!' Mim grunted. 'He can't expect to have glamour and talent. Now, I must dash. Have a good day tomorrow.'

Claire watched her friend depart and as the evening progressed wished she could come up with an excuse for not going on the walk herself, but she liked Mike too much to let him down, although inwardly she cursed him when she woke next morning at twenty minutes past eight. It was all rush and go to get to the agreed point by nine o'clock, and after forgetting that Miriam's sandwiches were in her fridge and having to return for them, she found that it was almost nine-fifteen when she pulled into the deserted car-park of the Lakeside Inn, some five miles away.

It was only then that she paused long enough to think about the weather. It had rained overnight, now there was a gloomy mist shrouding everything and it felt quite chilly. She got out of the car and looked about her, but the damp hung in curtains over the valley as she viewed it from the stone wall surrounding the inn's car-park. Trust me, she thought irritably, to be the only one to turn up, or had the others gone on already? That was doubtful. Mike had said nine for nine-thirty, and even that was early for a Sunday morning. She kept looking at her watch; there was a dismal solitude about the place, and even the birds seemed to be having a Sunday morning lie-in.

Feeling peeved that she appeared to be the only stupid member of the staff—Mike had evidently called it off and not had the presence of mind to ring her—Claire got back into her car. She switched on the radio, hoping to hear the time and the local weather forecast, and decided to wait until nine-thirty before returning home.

No weather forecast, only absurdly loud pop music to ravage her senses on a quiet Sunday morning, and then the crunch of tyres on the gravel, and in the mirror Claire watched as the sleek Granada purred to a standstill in the centre of the car-park. Oh no, she groaned, not Alan Jarvis and his wife! But as she observed with keen eyes and a pounding heart, a strangely clothed figure alighted from the passenger seat, went to the boot and extracted a rucksack, then waved to the driver who revved up and spun round, leaving the lone figure staring straight into Claire's mirror through the rear window.

Claire felt her temperature rising and falling in rapid succession, but she managed to keep her fingers steady as she switched off the radio and wound her window down.

'Good morning, Claire.' Alan Jarvis's face filled the

open space.

'Not such a good morning,' Claire replied levelly. 'I presume the walk has been called off?'

'Surely not—for what reason?' Alan looked surprised.

Claire raised her eyebrows towards the valley.

'The weather maybe?' she hinted.

'Just Spring mist,' he assured her. 'It'll be glorious later on. I understood from Mike that there would be about twenty or thirty coming along.'

Claire laughed. 'That was wishful thinking on Mike's part—especially if he put everyone else's name down on the list as he did Miriam's and mine. Probably half the staff don't even know they were supposed to come. Usually we only get about a dozen.'

'So you do this sort of thing quite often?'

Claire pursed her lips. 'Not often as an arranged outing—I do a fair bit of walking.'

'Good, then you can see that I don't get lost.'

'Oh, but I was just——' Claire began.

'Going home?—not on your life, my girl.' He opened her door and stood waiting for her to move.

Claire was covered in confusion. All sorts of empty excuses flashed through her brain, but being by nature a truthful person she voiced none of them. In fact she could think of nothing to say as she got out of the car and looked around. Where was Mike? Damn him—or at least a few of the staff who had arranged to come on the walk?

'Surely Mike would have let you know if it had been cancelled?' Alan suggested in answer to Claire's puzzled expression. 'I only got back late last night, so I haven't been to the hospital or seen anyone.'

Claire was surprised that a consultant should want to join the lesser staff of the hospital on a walk, and also was tempted to suggest he was lowering his standards by not rushing straight to Moorlands to see how the Wilsons were.

'Perhaps Mike has been put off by the weather,' Claire said hopefully looking up at the sky.

'But it's not going to put us off is it, Claire? After a few days of involvement in a conference in London I need some country air. Fiona's quite indignant at having to return, she loves London.'

'Couldn't you have persuaded her to walk with you?'

Alan threw his head back and laughed outright.

'Fiona—walking? She'd be a liability. Come along, let's get started—it's obvious no one else is going to turn up now.'

'But . . . the food,' Claire stammered, anything to delay setting off with Alan alone.

'I hear you're an expert pastry cook, I'm sure I can do it justice,' he said with an amused grin.

'But I've got masses,' she said lamely, 'and Mim did two loaves of sandwiches.'

'Excellent—if we get lost we shan't starve. Where is Miriam, by the way?'

Claire explained, and instead of being sympathetic Alan Jarvis seemed to find that amusing too.

'So there's nothing to keep us, Claire,' he said firmly. 'A challenge, my dear, we aren't going to let a little mist spoil our day.'

Claire hesitated; she was all for going home, but Alan had come dressed for the part of hiker with a padded jacket, boots, brown cords and a woolly hat complete with bobble. She couldn't take the risk of him going off alone and getting lost if he was new to the area.

'Do you know the dales?' she asked him.

He grinned boyishly. 'Hardly, since I did most of my training in London, and more recently worked in the States. But I'll take the risk of you showing me the ropes. You seem like a sensible girl.' He was sending her up.

'It really isn't sensible to start off in a mist,' she said, trying to sound competent.

He took her elbow in his hand and led her to the boot of her car. 'The food,' he ordered abruptly. 'Never turn down a challenge, Claire.'

Claire took out her own rucksack and Alan helped her on with it.

'I've brought a flask of coffee,' he informed her. 'I hate canned drinks—there should be enough for two.'

There was a smugness in his tone. He's enjoying this, Claire thought, so, what the heck? I might as well go along with him. Who cares about Fiona, if she is careless enough to let her man off the hook for a day!

Fumbling with the lock of her car she dropped the keys. Alan quickly picked them up, then pushed her out of the way with an impatient sigh as he fitted it into the lock and secured her car.

'Stop playing for time,' he said in mock reproach. 'You can't dislike me that much—or is it that you're afraid of what the grapevine is going to make of this?'

'Who's going to tell them?' Claire retorted haughtily.

Alan gave her a disconcerting look. 'If that's the way you want it, Claire—come on, which way?'

'There's a gate to the path at the side of the inn.'

'About a ten-mile walk, I believe Mike said?'

'We don't have to go that far,' Claire said quickly, 'but Finchdale Force is well worth seeing, especially after heavy rain.'

He fell into step beside her after passing through the gate. 'We haven't had much of that of late, but it has rained a little through the night. I think it will clear up again quite soon.'

He was right. As they walked through a beautiful green valley the mist suddenly cleared and the sun shone down warm and invigorating. They paused on the bridge by an old mill to look down into the rippling water as it chortled over the small rocks, and Claire experienced a light-headed feeling that all was well with the world. It didn't matter who she was with, just being away from the pressures of Moorlands and in open country was tonic enough for her.

It was about midday, after they had been walking up the Finchfigg Fell, sometimes scrambling to gain the height of well over one thousand feet, when Alan suggested they should rest a while.

As Claire slipped off her rucksack Alan spread a ground-sheet on a patch of soft green turf. She had to admit if only to herself that Alan was a most congenial companion, and as they sat together he pouring coffee, Claire delving into the boxes to find sandwiches or pastries she knew she was glad that Alan had not allowed her to return home. Like herself, he proved himself to be a nature lover. He was informative and knowledgeable about birds, flowers and everything that they came across in the wild, sometimes rugged countryside, but as impressed as Claire when they stopped to look down, or around them to admire the distant mountains, now clearly visible with the blue sky reflected in the lakes and smaller tarns below. They found a few late daffodils among an effusion of bluebells in a picturesque glen, and rhododendrons provided rich colour against the fresh green leaves of numerous trees. Occasionally they met other walkers but now, in a sheltered spot close to huge rocks between which thundered the waters of Finchdale Force, they were completely isolated.

They laughed together at the abundance of food for just the two of them, and Claire thought how absurdly youthful Alan appeared when he removed his bobble cap to show off his unruly mop of reddish-brown hair, a vastly different image from the Orthopaedic Consultant's.

'I told you it would be a lovely day, Claire,' he said with self-satisfaction. 'Aren't you glad you came?'

She nodded as if just to please him. 'Mm,' she mumbled between mouthfuls of one of Miriam's sandwiches.

'Not such an ogre after all, am I?' he teased.

Claire didn't answer. Up to now the conversation as they had walked together had been impersonal, but now she was suddenly reminded of the scene in her office just a week ago.

She glanced across at him and saw that he was raking over the mould of her breasts beneath the tight-fitting tee-shirt. Walking had invigorated her and feeling warm when they sat down, she had discarded her thick sweater.

Her simple tee-shirt was bright blue with a wide V-neck and cap sleeves. She felt her colour deepening knowing that her full pointed breasts, the envy of many of her friends, had attracted Alan's astute observations, and she wished that she had kept her sweater on, no matter how hot she was.

'Tell me about yourself, Claire, your family?' he invited casually.

Claire quickly drew her knees up to her chin, one hand gently clasped round the other wrist, her eyes scanning the distant horizon, as she bit off mouthfuls of her sandwich.

'Nothing much to tell,' she answered vaguely.

'Parents?—brothers?—sisters?' Alan asked.

Claire emptied her mouth thoughtfully.

'My mother died when I was eleven,' she said matter-of-factly.

'I'm sorry,' Alan sympathised. 'Has it made a difference to your life?'

Claire shrugged. 'I suppose so—but who knows in what way? My father married again, but not for five years. I think it might have been easier if he'd done it straight away. She was his secretary—they'd always been close, so I don't know why they thought it necessary to wait so long. Mother had a brain tumour, it was very sudden. My father seemed to think I would accept a stepmother more easily at sixteen.'

'But you didn't?'

'Yes. I'd always admired Rosemary—we got on well together.'

'But as a teenager you began to feel an intruder?'

Claire turned and looked at him quickly, surprised by his astuteness.

'Teenagers are vulnerable, Claire,' he went on seriously, 'susceptible to atmosphere. I expect your feelings were those of any other sixteen-year-old in similar circumstances.'

'I didn't rebel,' she began in self-examination.

'You're not the type.' His hand touched her cheek sending a warm glow through her.

'Don't you believe it,' she said rashly. 'Nursing, and learning to be independent, has changed me.'

'For the better I'm sure. Women are always more exciting if they have an insurgent streak.'

Claire didn't reply, and when Alan handed her a mug of coffee their hands momentarily touched.

It wasn't a thrill, of course not, she chided herself, but all the same it felt as if someone were plucking the vital cord of her nervous system.

'No brothers or sisters?' Alan asked.

'One brother four years younger than me, two half-sisters and a half-brother—and it was when they came along that I began to feel the odd one out. It wasn't my parents' fault, and my father never knew how I felt. Maybe I let the jealousy—if that is what it was—grow out of all proportion. To try to please Father I just put everything I'd got into studying. I wanted to be a doctor, would you believe—but I didn't quite make the grade.'

'You should have tried again, Claire,' Alan said eagerly.

'I settled for nursing, and I'm content with my lot. My kid brother, Malcolm, he's going to be the doctor of the family. He's at university now. Strangely enough, we've become even closer as he's grown older.'

'That's nice—but by the time he qualifies you'll be married with a family.'

'Oh yes?' Claire retorted sarcastically. 'Is that a promise?'

Alan laughed, and ruffled her hair. 'You've got everything going for you—when we get beneath the prickly Sister image.'

'I haven't got that sort of image,' Claire argued hotly, then with a troubled expression: 'Have I?'

Alan had been lying on his side, propped up on one elbow. Now, with a swift movement he pulled her down beside him, teasing her, ending the frivolity with a quick kiss.

Claire sat up again, shrugging off any embarrassment by brushing crumbs from her jeans. If he thought she was easy game for that kind of horseplay just because they were alone together, he could think again. But, of course, she supposed, he was just trying to make her feel at ease.

'Richard Lynch seems to have found the recipe to get beneath the starch,' Alan said drily.

'Any interest I've shown in Mr Lynch is simply to try to persuade him to be less inhibited,' Claire returned adamantly, wishing that he hadn't reminded her of Richard at that precise moment.

'He doesn't seem very inhibited to me,' Alan responded. 'You didn't need to take it quite so far, Claire, and you know as well as I do that you wouldn't have done if you didn't feel some attraction towards him.'

'Attraction!' Claire pursed her lips impatiently. 'Mm— I quite like him—and he's a lonely man,' she excused.

'You took an interest in him as a patient. He was flattered by your attention and responded as any normal man would do. You in turn are flattered now by his appeal. Be careful, Claire. We know so little about him—

he *was* married, so he says—you don't want to get caught up in some cheap affair.'

Claire turned on him with eyes blazing.

'How do you know what I want?' she answered back shortly. 'And we are off duty—do we have to discuss the patients?'

'No,' Alan submitted calmly. 'I wasn't discussing my patients, I was talking about you.'

'Then let's drop the subject—if you have any complaints about my work, or behaviour while on duty, you know where to go with them.'

He gripped her arm tightly. 'I hope for your sake that will never be necessary, my dear. I'm just warning you to take care—it's up to you to make sure that you don't get too involved.'

'Let me go,' she cried angrily trying to shake off his hold. 'If I get involved that's my affair. You aren't consultant over my private life,' she added childishly.

'At least have a little decent self-respect, Claire. Your work is a reflection of your private life, and I don't want to see you make a fool of yourself.'

'If I do it won't be anything to do with you, and I'm sure my work won't suffer.'

'You're not only a stubborn little fool, you're pig-headed as well. You're old enough to know what a few seemingly harmless kisses can lead to.'

With a violent tug she pulled free and struggled to her feet.

'So?' she demanded, angered even more by the cool gaze in his dark eyes. 'What's your game, then?'

There was no immediate reaction—when it did come it was so swift and aggressive that he caught Claire off balance. She didn't know what he did to the back of her knees but they went weak, and she found herself down on the ground-sheet, held captive in his arms. He looked into her face, his body shielding hers, one leg forcing hers into obedience.

'There's a subtle difference, Claire—*I* have the right,' he said with determination, and his mouth settled fiercely over hers until her body went limp in surrender.

She wanted to scream at him. What rights had *he*—already married to the gorgeous Fiona? Not even as much right as Richard, she thought petulantly, but she had no chance to express her thoughts as his mouth sensuously tempered her obstinacy. It was useless to struggle against his powerful muscles. A little voice inside her head was telling her that she should be at least opposing his compulsion, but he knew how to use his skills effectively, and she lay inert beneath his hungry passion, her bosom urged against his masculine chest.

She felt his fingers gentle and persuasive searching for the top of her jeans and for a moment panic seized her, but he stifled her cries with a probing tongue, his warm touch exciting her naked flesh beneath her tee-shirt. His hand crept upwards to caress her breasts while his mouth travelled a dreamy pathway over her eyes and cheeks, taking an animal nibble at her earlobes before coming back to her mouth, and the second before his lips touched hers he paused to gaze into the brilliant blue of her eyes.

The dark velvet depths of his were brimming with desire and Claire was aware of a pulse in her neck throbbing violently.

'We could do without all this,' he whispered huskily, tussling with her clothes.

'No, Alan—please—not here,' she begged, but he ignored her and pushed her tee-shirt up to expose the front of her. She cursed the fact that her bra had a front fastening which he took as an open invitation to undo and explore the smooth white skin of her full breasts. He investigated with fingers and lips and appeared to be unaware of her attempts to struggle, and wriggle her body from beneath his weight.

She appreciated his devious cleverness as her struggles gave way to sensual movement, and she was unable to stifle a moan of pleasure at his petting, especially when his slender fingers undid the zip on her jeans. Flesh against flesh, stimulating and yet agonising, his lips following the track of his fingertips over the delicious curves and hollows of her body, causing an ecstasy so breathtaking that her body lifted spontaneously—and then a giggle brought an abrupt end to the pleasure.

Flushed with guilt, Claire pushed her tee-shirt down. She could hardly believe her ears when Alan abused the onlooker, a young lad in his early teens, with a string of unrepeatable expletives. For a few seconds the lad, eagerly joined by two of his friends stared on impudently until Alan got to his feet and chased them away. With shrieks of defiant glee they made off, and Alan came up behind Claire, who was rearranging her clothes. He nuzzled her neck and with dexterity helped her to zip up her jeans.

'That was unfortunate,' he whispered in her ear, but for Claire the magic had evaporated. Alan Jarvis was playing games with her, whiling away a Sunday afternoon and after all he had said about getting involved with Richard. Claire was furious, not only with him, but with herself for allowing him to catch her like a helpless butterfly in a net. She knelt down and began packing up the remnants of their picnic lunch, but Alan placed his hands underneath her armpits and lifted her to her feet.

'Come on, darling,' he said persuasively, 'you can't let a slight interruption quell such passion.'

'You save your passion for Fiona,' Claire flung at him. 'It's time we started back.'

'My God,' he answered, dark brows meeting in frustrated rancour, 'you can certainly change your mood quickly. What's the matter—scared?' he taunted.

She swung out of his grasp.

'Not of you,' she fumed, 'but I didn't come on this fell walk for the reasons you have in mind.'

He took a step nearer so that he towered over her, hands at his waist inside his open jacket. She was forced to look away from the smouldering heat in his eyes, and God, how the sight of his rippling muscles beneath his knitted shirt and the matt of rich golden hair visible in the opening made her go weak all over again!

'You aren't any different from any other woman,' he yelled at her. 'I'd cracked the chink in your starchy armour, hadn't I? Another few minutes——'

'And I'd have slapped your face,' she shouted, incensed at his arrogance.

Now he sneered, his lips curling in contempt.

'Go on, then—and see what you get back, my girl. Just because a couple of peeping Toms taunt you, you want to run off home and weep tears of shame. I thought you said you did a lot of walking—we've hardly begun yet. The word "fell" means the ground between seven hundred feet and the top of a mountain.' He pointed to a higher peak. 'That was the target, wasn't it? Finchfigg Ridge —nearly three thousand feet—no stamina, that's your trouble.'

'My stamina is as good as yours,' she argued hotly.

'Then what are we waiting for? We'll see the Force first.'

He zipped up his jacket, replaced his bobble-cap and secured his rucksack, then turned to watch Claire struggling with hers, which she did with trembling fingers. She'd show him, insufferable swine. She'd tire him out and prove who was the better hiker.

CHAPTER SEVEN

They walked side by side, at a good pace but emotionally oceans apart.

Alan was like all men, Claire thought, out for what he could get and disappointed when he didn't get it. Out in the open, too—what sort of animal was he beneath that smooth exterior? She trudged on beside him aware that he didn't intend to make any allowances for her because she was a mere woman, or the fact that she was so much shorter than he.

The rumblings of falling water grew louder as they neared the waterfalls which could be heard some distance away. Alan went ahead along a narrow track until they reached the rocky parapet, and there, tumbling down from some seventy feet was the gushing torrent, the roar of which made conversation impossible.

It was an impressive sight and they stood in awe of the gigantic force as well as the picturesque surroundings where the water fell over boulders and rocks, and beyond disappearing from view into a leafy glen.

At last Alan grabbed Claire's hand to pull her away and back on to the narrow footpath, where he pointed to the higher mountain ridge. Neither of them spoke, but Claire knew that he meant to test her skill and stamina. The higher they climbed the more difficult it was to breathe, and as the time passed by, so intent did they become in their private battle of endurance that they were oblivious to the fact that their goal had become screened in mist.

Alan was well ahead of her when Claire suddenly looked up in alarm, then to the back of the distant figure of Alan, fast disappearing into the damp net of gloom. He must have noticed, she thought spitefully, yet he's deliberately going on. Stubbornness prevented her from calling to him; she just kept going.

She came up against him abruptly and he glowered down at her.

'Keep up or you'll get lost,' he said, and with that he strode on determinedly.

Claire wanted to suggest that they turn back but that would be giving in. She had been to the top of Finchfigg once before and remembered that it was possible to come down on the other side, the path gradually winding round so that you reached the point at which you started, but Lakeside Inn suddenly seemed a long way off, and again she seemed to have lagged behind.

'Keep up,' Alan shouted. 'It's narrow through here—I don't want you going over the edge. If we'd got up here earlier the mist wouldn't have obscured the scenery. I believe you can see a great panoramic view of several lakes and peaks in the area from here.'

Claire felt like retorting that any time loss was entirely due to his indulgences; she also wondered where he got so much information from. Probably Mike, who would have been anxious to get the consultant interested. Damn and blast Mike Boyd, Claire thought aggressively. If it weren't for him she would be at home relaxing instead of blindly following the austere Alan Jarvis.

The last bit of the climb to the summit was the most difficult. The dampness underfoot on the craggy ground caused her to slip and slide as well as panting for breath. She felt she just couldn't go on; every ounce of strength was being drained from her. She didn't care where *he* was—over the side of the precipice for all she cared, and each time she saw what must be the top path it was only to discover a few more rocks or boulders to scramble over, and with every breath she vowed she couldn't take one more step.

Her cheeks felt cinder-hot, her eyes bulging, her body aching with weariness—never again, she declared, *never!*

She found a hand-hold over a sharp rock, this must surely be the top. She heaved and her foot slipped, she flayed about wildly with her legs searching for a firm stand, but her hand then began to slip off the rock above. She wasn't aware of shouting, she didn't think she had the breath to utter any noise, but a firm grasp prevented her from slipping any further and Alan hauled her to safety where she lay panting. She wanted to weep from exhaustion but his cruel laugh made her struggle to her feet, and wielding what little strength she had, she hurled herself at him.

'You hateful beast,' she yelled as he caught her forearms and held her off.

'Stop it, Claire, at once,' he said sternly. 'You've brought it on yourself, and if I were anything but a gentleman I'd call you a stupid, obstinate cow. Your suffering over the last hour has been of your own volition, you had only to say that you'd had enough.'

'Enough!' Claire screamed wildly. 'I've had enough of *you*, and this blasted walk.' The tears of anguish were falling fast now, and she didn't care. 'I want to go home,' she sobbed.

He held her arms more tightly, and gently shook her.

'Just calm down,' he said firmly, 'and don't waste your breath blaming me, or crying like a schoolgirl.'

He let her go and she blew her nose and dried her eyes with a tissue. 'We should have turned back ages ago,' she said submissively.

'This is only the Lake District, not the jungle, and we haven't been pot-holing. Every road has to lead to somewhere. According to my map which I studied in detail last evening, this narrow ridge widens into a descending path, and I have no doubt that as we go along we shall find ourselves beneath the mist.' He caught her chin in his hand. 'You don't really think I'd lose you, do you?'

'But you don't know the area.'

'Neither, it seems, do you,' he replied sarcastically. 'Now hold on to the belt of my jacket until we get along the ridge. Thank goodness it doesn't get dark too early.'

'Shouldn't we go back the way we came?' Claire suggested meekly.

'Certainly not—and if you're going to behave like a baby then I shall ditch you.'

Reluctantly she did as she was told, holding on to his belt, treading in his footsteps, and as they came to a steep descent he used his weight to prevent her from going too fast. He'd been wrong about one thing at least, because the mist descended all the way with them. But they soon came to a wider pathway where they could walk side by side, and as they walked through a thickly wooded area they could hear rushing water again.

'That'll be Finchbeck Falls,' Alan said, and when they drew nearer, guided by the sound, they found some wooden seats and a flat area suitably arranged for tourists.

'We'll take a rest here, at least there are makeshift conveniences which are better than getting lost in the bushes. You never know there might even be a light.'

Claire found that there was, and a water tap so that she could wipe her face over, which helped her to feel human again.

'Come on, let's have our tea,' Alan said, when she joined him on a seat.

'No—let's get on or it will be dark.'

But he pulled her to him roughly and removed her rucksack. 'You can't go on for ever without eating. It will give you some added vigour.'

She opened the packages and boxes and found that she was really quite hungry. It must be hours since they had eaten their lunch, and hours, she thought dismally, until they would reach Lakeside Inn again. At least the walk had been planned from there rather than Moorlands, which was something to be thankful for.

They set off again, Alan jauntily, Claire not at all happy with the way things had turned out, but he held her hand protectively, and as darkness closed in with the mist she was glad of his assurance.

Through a glen and encircling a small lake they came to a fork in the road.

'To the left,' Alan decided.

'To the right, surely?' Claire differed.

'This way,' Alan insisted but Claire pulled to the right.

'Don't be tiresome, there's a good girl,' Alan said as if speaking to a schoolgirl.

'*I'm* going right,' she insisted. 'The left-hand fork will only take you farther away.'

'Don't be absurd, Claire.'

'You go where you like,' she admonished, 'but I don't want to get lost.'

He grabbed her wrist and pull as she might he forced her along beside him.

'Listen,' she begged, 'it's common sense——'

'It's common sense, darling, to admit that we are lost,' he said pointedly.

Claire didn't appreciate his statement for a moment then she rounded on him fiercely. 'It's all your damned fault,' she accused. 'Why can't we try my way?'

'I thought you'd been walking before?'

'I have, but only to the top of Finchfigg on one occasion. It's some climb.'

He gazed down at her with a wicked smile.

'I know, but we did it, didn't we?' he said softly.

'What's the point of taking this road if it's wrong?'

'Every road has its end, darling, and at least this one seems to be sloping downwards. Yours began to wind up again.'

'How could you tell?—we can't see in the dark—you're just guessing.'

'All right, so I'm guessing. This way has to bring us to a village.'

Claire walked beside him disconsolately and after what seemed hours later the road petered out into open moorland. The trek was never-ending, and any landmarks were reached by accident, huge pre-historic stone circles, burial mounds and earthworks.

'We must come to a signpost soon,' Claire moaned, thirsty as well as weary and footsore.

'You're not worried, are you?' he taunted.

'Tired,' she answered flatly.

'We may have to bed down for the night in any shelter we can find.'

'We keep going,' Claire retorted, and quickened her pace.

They came to a stone wall which Alan spanned easily.

'It must mean civilisation,' he said cheerfully.

Claire eagerly climbed on to the top of the wall, and as she scaled the other side let out a piercing wail. Apart from the acute pain on the inside of her thigh she heard her jeans rip ominously.

Alan supported her anxiously to the ground.

'What is it, Claire?—what have you done?'

'Torn my jeans, and my leg inside them by the feel of it. There must have been barbed wire on this side of the wall.'

Alan took a small torch out of his pocket.

'Good grief,' Claire exclaimed. 'Do you mean to tell me you came all prepared? That we've been struggling along in the dark when all the time you had a torch?'

'Only a small one—which I was saving for obvious reasons.' He flashed the light over Claire. 'Just as well I did come prepared—take off your jeans.'

'Certainly not,' she exploded.

'You're bleeding, Claire, and if I bandage over the top it will all stick together.'

'So let it all stick together. It isn't that bad.'

Alan flashed his torch on the wall.

'Rusty barbed wire—very dangerous. Out of those jeans and no arguments!'

He took off his rucksack to take out the ground-sheet but Claire set off, hobbling over the rough ground. She knew he was following because he was calling, and in a few minutes he caught up with her.

'You're the most maddening woman I've ever come across,' he said angrily.

'There's no point in stopping now,' she said.

'And I can't let you go on in that state. At least take off those filthy jeans and let me look.'

'My jeans are not filthy,' she said indignantly. 'They were clean on this morning.'

'They're filthy now.'

'I want to go on.'

'But you're bleeding.'

'Not much, it'll soon stop.'

She didn't know what sort of hold he used, but the next minute she was flat on her back. The fight had gone out of her and she lay still as he eased her jeans down gently, grumbling all the time.

'Stupid tight things to wear,' he muttered crossly. 'Why didn't you wear something warm and sensible?'

'Because I didn't expect to be out all night,' she answered back.

With a gentle touch he dabbed some liquid from a small bottle on to the long jagged wound, then bound up her leg using a whole length of bandage.

'We shall have to find a sheltered spot for the night—build a fire and all that.'

'Not on your life,' Claire replied sharply, and drew her jeans back up quickly.

'Stubborn as a mule,' he complained as she stood up and folded up the ground-sheet.

They walked on, Alan carefully pacing his steps to hers, but Claire knew she would not be able to go much farther. By the sticky mess between her legs she knew that her leg was bleeding badly, and walking was only aggravating the situation. Her steps grew slower as her condition became more uncomfortable.

Suddenly Alan shouted, 'Look—a light!'

The mist was miraculously clearing and below them in a hollow, a welcoming light shone out to greet them.

It urged Claire forward and when they came to another stone wall Claire leant against it thankfully.

'Perhaps they've got a phone—we could get Mike to come out to meet us,' she said hopefully.

'It's after ten o'clock and he'll be on call. The best we can hope for is a bed for the night,' Alan said. 'I'll go on and see what joy I get—you sit by the wall and *don't move*,' he commanded.

Hysterics overcame Claire while he was gone. What a situation to be in, she thought. Alone with a man whom she disliked intensely, yet who caused her inner feelings a great deal of bother.

Alan seemed to be gone for ages. They couldn't be that far away if her sense of direction served her correctly, and she'd never got lost before. She had never gone walking before in even the slightest mist, she remembered with a touch of sourness. She certainly wouldn't have ventured far today if Alan hadn't persuaded her.

Not so much persuaded as ordered, she reflected without humour. He was an infuriating man who so subtly engineered having his own way in everything. In future she would be on her guard, she decided. She should have known better than to set off with him alone, but it had been enjoyable for part of the day. She was angry with herself for not sticking to her guns and turning back after lunch. It was too late now for recriminations. She was here, somewhere in the Cumbrian dales with an unpleasant wound on her inner thigh, and, she realised, shelter in a barn would be better than nothing.

As the mist cleared, so the moon illuminated the countryside casting pale moonglow over the hedgerows and trees. Claire felt extremely isolated and reluctantly wished that Alan would return. She could make out some buildings in the distance and thought she could hear a dog barking. Somewhere overhead an owl hooted making her jump, and the leaves rustled when the wind agitated them, setting up an eerie moan in the night air. A light attracted her attention. She heard a door slam and then saw a pinpoint of light waving on the horizon, coming slowly towards her.

Alan reached her swiftly; his slowness was only an illusion, Claire conceded appreciatively.

'It's a farmhouse—they've got room for us. I've explained that I'm a doctor and that you're hurt,' he said. 'How's the leg?'

'All right,' Claire answered, but she couldn't disguise the wince of pain when she stood up.

'Shall I carry you and come back for the rucksacks?' Alan suggested.

'No—I'll manage, but it's awkward on this rough ground.'

'There's a path soon, it'll be easier then. Put your arm through mine and lean towards me.'

'My jeans are rubbing—it feels a mess.'

'I'll soon have you cleaned up—come along.'

The farmhouse itself was much nearer than Claire had suspected, and as soon as they approached the back door it was flung open and a man came out to help Alan with the rucksacks and Claire saw a small, round, elderly woman framed in the doorway.

'Can you manage, Doctor?' she asked as without any

warning Alan swung Claire up into his arms.

'Fine thanks. I'll take her straight up,' he said.

'There's plenty of hot water, sir, and I've already put the first aid box in the room.'

Alan made to place Claire on the bed in the large, comfortably decorated room. The ceiling was low, and chintzy curtains covered the window alcove. One bar of an electric fire sent a cheering warmth towards Claire as she clung to Alan.

'Not on the bed,' she pleaded, 'I'm all bloody.'

He gently allowed her to stand close to the wash-hand basin in one corner of the room.

'I'll be okay, Alan, really,' Claire said, willing him out of the room.

'Your modesty does you credit, darling,' he began but was interrupted by the farmer's wife appearing in the doorway.

'Have you got everything you want for your good lady, sir?' she asked. 'I've got plenty of old, clean linen.'

'That might be a good idea to save messing up your bedding,' Alan agreed, and took the neat pile of folded towels and tea towels from her.

'Some hot soup? A drink—what would you like, sir?'

'I think a tray of tea would be greatly appreciated, Mrs Barstow, and—brandy?' he queried.

'Of course, Doctor, right away.'

She went away and closed the door. Alan rolled back the bedcovers and spread out a couple of large old towels, then he turned to Claire. She met his gaze fearlessly, trying to hide the tremor of fear which had coursed through her veins.

'I can manage, thank you,' she said icily.

Alan spread his hands in a gesture of helplessness.

'Sorry, darling—she had only one room to spare. They're a large family. Four strapping sons, she said.'

'What did she mean "your good lady"?' Claire asked

tightly.

'For God's sake, Claire, don't be naïve. Play the game, it's only for one night. I had to pretend you were my wife.'

'You rotten pig!' Claire yelled. 'You should have told her the truth—*you* could have slept on a couch somewhere.'

'Oh, thank you very much. I'm just as weary as you are. Now stop your whining and get out of those jeans.'

His fingers were at her zip before she could protest.

He smacked her hands away sharply.

'For tonight, Claire Tyndall, you're my wife—love, honour and *obey*.'

Claire clawed at him and stamped her foot angrily; the wrong one, so that her frenzy was short-lived as the pain shot through her leg.

'You're hateful, despicable—I don't want you to touch me,' she said in despair.

He glanced up at her scornfully. 'Too bad. If you play up I shall put you across my knee, so just quieten down and do as you're told.'

She lifted one foot at a time as he removed each shoe and then pulled off her jeans. She had been so busy protesting that she hadn't been aware of him easing the torn jeans away from the nasty gash in her leg.

Now that she stood there in briefs and short socks she found herself trembling uncontrollably. She tugged at her baggy sweater, glad that it covered her hips and thighs.

After taking off his own jacket Alan lifted her and placed her on the bed on the towels, then with deft fingers pushed the sweater up to her waist and parted her legs. The bandage was stuck, and Claire covered her face with her hands as Alan began to ease it away from the wound.

'Sorry, darling,' he whispered kindly. 'I'll try not to hurt you too much, but I must get it off.'

She heard him go to the basin and fill it, then she felt his gentle fingers sponging away the messy bandage. She bit on her handkerchief until it was freed. His touch was so damnably light on her skin that she tingled all over.

'I could have done it myself,' Claire said half-apologetically.

'While you have a doctor husband you may as well make the most of him.' He was bathing the wound carefully then cleaning up all around the top of her leg and right down to her sock where the blood had trickled. 'I don't get many opportunities to render first aid. By the time the patient reaches me it's all been done.'

A light tap at the door brought Mrs Barstow back into the room.

'This will bring back some life,' she said heartily as she placed a tray on the table near a huge easy chair.

'I must compliment you, Mrs Barstow, on a very well-equipped first aid box,' Alan congratulated her.

'It's necessary on a busy farm,' she said. 'Are you sure you have all you need, Dr Jarvis?'

'Yes, indeed. The bleeding has stopped, but I'll bind it up well for the night.'

Mrs Barstow left the room, and Alan covered Claire's wound with a large piece of lint, then two layers of gauze and a strong crêpe bandage from thigh to knee.

'How does that feel?' he asked with a smile.

'Okay,' she said, sitting up and pulling her sweater down again.

'Only "okay"?' he mocked. 'Don't overdo the praise, will you?'

'You don't deserve any,' she retorted. 'I don't like people who do things under false pretences. You could have consulted me—asked me whether I minded or not.'

'There wasn't much alternative—and for heaven's sake stop putting on an act of injustice. You women are all the same. You practically throw yourself at a man, beg him to make love to you, and when he does you promptly accuse him of rape.'

'I have not thrown myself at you,' she replied savagely, 'nor accused you of rape—yet. I didn't want to come on this blasted walk anyway, and certainly not with you alone.'

Alan put his arm around her shoulders and helped her across to the table.

'But it wasn't all bad was it?—and it might even get better—we've got all night,' he said provocatively. 'Come on, have a sip of brandy to warm you up.'

'I suppose you think that's a sure way of getting what you want?' she said recklessly.

'I can do that, darling, without the help of brandy, believe me. But seeing that you're such a modest, starchy Sister you can have the bed all to yourself. The easy chair—even the floor—will do me tonight. But don't get careless; you can't be sure you're absolutely safe. I mean, all that walking can only stimulate a virile man like myself. It's a bit much to expect me to behave myself when I have the tantalising prospect of spending the next ten hours with a quite beautiful girl—when she isn't playing at "Sisters", that is.'

'You're contemptible,' she said between her teeth.

Alan laughed. 'And you're lovely when you're angry. Scarlet cheeks, flashing blue eyes and definitely at a disadvantage being half-naked.'

Claire was too concerned about her state of undress to argue further. She replaced the glass on the tray and limped across to the chair where Alan had hung her jeans.

'What a mess,' she murmured half to herself, half to the tattered jeans.

'Perhaps Mrs Barstow would have needle and thread,' Alan suggested.

'Do you think she might? Would she mind?' Claire

wondered, turning and facing Alan who had made himself comfortable in the easy chair and was drinking tea, appraising her from over the rim of the cup. He smiled.

'You look good like that, Claire. Better without the socks and bandage—definitely a provocative new look.'

'I wasn't aiming to please anyone or introduce a new fashion. I shall just have to wear my jeans as they are,' she said dismally.

'Just because you're sharing a room with a man doesn't mean you have to stay fully dressed all night. Come and drink your tea, then when I go down to use the telephone I'll see if Mrs Barstow has suitable needle and thread.'

'If there's a telephone here, why didn't you ring for a taxi to take us back to the Lakeside Inn? It wouldn't be any more expensive than putting up here,' Claire said irritably, returning to the table to fetch her cup of tea.

'Because there are no taxis in the area. This happens to be an isolated farm. All right—I'd better come clean, I suppose. I said I didn't know the district, but only because it's years since I was here. I was actually born not far from Moorlands.'

'But you still got lost,' Claire reminded him bitterly.

'I said I haven't been back for—oh—twenty years. The family home, Birchdale, has been left to me by my grandfather, who died recently. My own parents couldn't get on with him, and moved to Scotland when I was a lad. Now they're comfortable where they are, so Birchdale has become my responsibility. I thought I had taken the road from Finchfigg which led down the mountain pass, through the village and to Birchdale, but according to Mrs Barstow we took the wrong pass when we actually left the waterfall.'

'It almost sounds as if you know the Barstows?' she accused.

'I only vaguely remember them. They knew my grandfather very well and remember me as a boy.'

'And you've told them we're married?' Claire asked incredulously. 'Supposing Fiona comes into contact with them?'

Alan laughed as he so often did when Fiona was mentioned. 'Most unlikely. Fiona won't ever go walking so will never reach this far, my dear. Don't worry, no one of importance need ever know about our little game. The Barstows, like most country people, are a little old-fashioned. I wouldn't like to offend them, which is why I thought it prudent to give us marital status.'

'But you've lied and cheated, which is much worse,' Claire said.

'That depends on your point of view. I consider it a little harmless deception, necessary to see that you were accommodated and your injury tended. Now—is there anyone you should inform of your whereabouts?'

'No—I live alone. Oh—my car! Jo Morrison, the landlord of Lakeside might get worried, if he isn't already.'

'You leave your car there frequently? or is Lakeside your "local"?'

'It's the hospital's local. Jo was a patient and in gratitude lets us use the car-park as a meeting place—well, lots of people do. He's in a good spot for starting walks, and coaches use it as a pick-up point too.'

'I'll give him a ring and tell him, also Mike so that he can cope until we return. When are you due back on duty?'

'Monday midday.' Colour flooded into Claire's cheeks guiltily as she wondered how on earth she was going to explain any of this to anyone, but Alan was prepared and read her thoughts.

'No need to think up alibis, Claire. We got lost, spent the night at a farmhouse, all perfectly true. No one needs to know we shared the same room. Indeed, no one *will* know unless you tell them.' He carried the tray to the door, leaving the brandy goblets on the table.

'I'll stay as long as I can. I suggest you hop into bed after you've done whatever you do before retiring.'

Claire needed to do very little, and soon she was snuggled beneath the sheets. It was useless to bemoan the fact that she had no toothbrush or flannel, no night attire, so that she was obliged to get into bed with most of her clothes on. The sweater was too much so she tossed that aside, and was glad she was wearing the tee-shirt underneath. Bra straps were likely to become abrasive as the night wore on, so she slipped that off too, and was sitting up sipping her brandy when Alan returned.

'Mrs Barstow has kindly offered to see what she can do to your jeans, darling,' he said, with a warning glance as Mrs Barstow hovered in the doorway. 'She says there's a school bus which will take us back to Birchdale village in the morning. It stops here at about quarter to nine.'

'That's good,' Claire managed to say in a friendly tone. 'But really, I can see to my jeans.'

'No trouble, Mrs Jarvis. I'm a dab hand at such things—been doing it all my life, and I cut up old ones to mend the next lot. Do it for my three grandchildren now—it's everyone to his trade. *I* couldn't nurse the sick—not more'n I have to at home.'

'I'm sorry we've put you to so much trouble,' Claire said.

'Bless you, my dear, 'tis no trouble. Glad to have company—we always keep a room for lost walkers. Get plenty in the summer, we do.'

She took the jeans from Alan, and in return gave him a bundle of pale green frothy material she'd been holding. 'Keep all kinds of spares too— don't be afraid to ask for anything. With a family my size—two of 'em married, and all living on the farm, I've gained the daughters I never had—and we can supply almost anything. You'll find new toothbrushes and flannels in the cupboard over the basin.'

Alan thanked her and closed the door after she had gone. He strolled casually to the foot of the bed and tossed the pale green nightdress to Claire.

'Better than nothing,' he said, with a touch of irony, then with a wicked grin: 'Depends whether you're the wearer or the critic, I suppose.' He returned to the door and Claire's expression must have readily registered hope but he turned, still wearing his wicked grin. 'I'm just going along the landing. Five minutes at most to give you time to brush your teeth and put the nightie on.'

Claire moved as speedily as her leg would allow her, first to try the nightdress for size, and it fitted to perfection. Not that there was that much of it to fit, she thought as she took stock of herself in a long wardrobe mirror. The bodice was little more than two triangles of see-through nylon which tapered into thin shoulder straps. Below the bustline the material was gathered into a wide waistband, and from there an effusion of material hung in folds, the long skirt having insertions of wide lace up to hip level. It was a delicate shade and quite becoming, she decided, certainly more comfortable than the tee-shirt and briefs.

When Alan returned to the room she was still fumbling to remove the wrapper from the toothbrush, but Alan ignored her, apparently finding the brandy more interesting than Claire.

She was surprised to find that he had peeled off his shirt when she turned again, and was seeking to extract one of the blankets.

'I suppose you don't mind if I have something to cover me for the night?' His eyes softened as he absorbed the vision in one swift glance before he continued to disarrange the bedclothes.

After that Claire was aware of a tense atmosphere, and neither of them spoke except when she had made herself comfortable in the huge bed, when Alan enquired how her leg was, and the final glimpse she had of him before he switched off the light was as he slipped off his trousers. Claire noticed that his back was broad, a healthy tan covering his fine muscular body, which moved with the grace of an agile jungle beast.

She waited expectantly, but he didn't even say goodnight, which gave her a feeling of inertia as she lay beneath the cool sheets. The brandy caused her blood to surge with fire so she had pushed back the eiderdown which Alan had refused. Sleep must surely come quickly she hoped, but the knowledge that she was in a comfortable bed while Alan was wrestling with the discomfort of an easy chair did nothing but keep her awake. She tried to condemn him for the situation in which she found herself, but the very sound of his breathing so close, yet so distant from her, made her restless. She tossed and turned having considerable space in which to do so, and at last realising that her head was higher than usual, giving her neck-ache, she pushed the fat bolster away from beneath her pillow.

Guilt at occupying a large bed alone made her uneasy even though there was little she could do about it, but eventually she relaxed and drifted off to sleep.

CHAPTER EIGHT

CLAIRE came to when it was still dark, hardly remembering where she was or what had happened during the past few hours. She snuggled deeper into the bed, her subconscious telling her she could have more hours of sleep if it was not yet light. She was pleasantly comfortable, warm, but not unduly so and she smiled secretly when she felt the flimsy nylon material covering her body, and wondered what Alan Jarvis would have thought if she'd told him that usually she didn't bother with such feminine creations. She lived alone and enjoyed her freedom in so many ways.

She hardly had time to consider his comfort or otherwise before she dozed off gradually to a deep slumber again. The kind of sleep that was dreamless, satisfying, completely relaxing, so it came as a surprise when, after slowly coming to her senses again, she felt the pressure of an arm across her waist.

Bit by bit her memory stirred to all that had taken place, and she stiffened with annoyance when she realised that it was Alan Jarvis's arm. His breathing was even, he was sleeping soundly, so she thought better of the attack she considered making on him. He deserved to have some rest, she decided with condescension, but wished he'd woken her so that they could have changed places. She became aware of the warmth of the human body which lay in the impression of her own. Now that she was really awake she could feel his heart gently beating a rhythmic pattern against her shoulder, and the downy growth of hair that thatched his chest brushed against her skin.

She realised with yet another shock that she found it agreeable to feel his nearness. This was such a different situation from the usual one she woke to at her own lonely flat. How many times had she day-dreamed of having a man to share her home with? A man to cook and clean for, a man to love. She remembered Karlotta's star-reading. The most unlikely and ineligible man was the one who would make her happy.

Then, like the dawn creeping up slowly and surely, Claire felt the truth becoming apparent. This man was the one she could really love. Her blood ran cold then hot by turns. She was afraid to move lest he moved, lest he took his arm away, and the gentleness of his pressure made her body ache with longing for him. She had fought him because it was the only way. It was still the only way, she remembered, because there was Fiona.

Stealthily she tried to edge away. Why, oh why, hadn't he left the big fat bolster between them? She felt the influence of his fingers holding her still, and his masculine body nestled even closer against hers. She held her breath as his hand slipped downwards on the soft nylon. She wished she had the courage to push the nightie down to its full length instead of having an untidy roll around her hips. She ought to restrain him, but his caress was sensual, and then his fingers travelled upwards until one breast was cupped in his hand.

Was he awake? Or was this how he lingered each morning half awake, half asleep beside the beautiful Fiona? Claire knew she should wake him—violently if need be—but as his thumb slid in regular recurrence over her nipple, she felt her whole being wakening to his demands. Her bosom swelled with delight to his manipulation until each breast was thrust into the strained triangles of nylon, and without meaning to she rolled on to her back and Alan eased his body over hers. She could feel the vibrations of his muscles, the hardness of uncontrollable lust against her, and she pushed her feet down in an effort to stay her own desire.

The minute covering over her breasts was of little consequence as Alan opened his eyes and gazed into her bright blue ones. His lips covering hers prevented any protest as he slid the shoulder straps over her arms and the nightie down to her ankles.

He must wake to the fact that I'm not Fiona, Claire thought, he must, he *must*, but his covetous dark eyes devoured every inch of her voluptuous body with hunger as he reviewed the length of her.

'Mm,' he whispered nuzzling his face into the hollow of her neck. 'It's Monday morning—I thought I only got spoilt on Sundays.'

Claire was mesmerised by his passion and linked her arms around his neck, kissing him back with a thirst for more.

'Delayed action,' she whsipered, and felt her body respond to his intimate loving.

As she ran her hands over his strong, smooth back his skin was like silk to her. There was no control over his sensitive touching whether with his fingers or lips, and it drove her to distraction. When he wove a course of intrigue from breast to breast and lower, enchanted by her feminine secrets, Claire allowed her fingers to play in his hair and behind his ears and the effect threatened destruction to both of them.

The knock on the door flashed between them like lightning, and Mrs Barstow mistook Alan's groan of frustration for an invitation to enter.

'Sorry to have to waken you, but if you want to catch the school bus I thought I'd best start you off with a cup of tea,' she said brightly.

Claire turned quickly on to her side, hiding her face with shame, feigning sleep. She felt Alan pull himself up in the bed taking the sheet with him so that their nakedness was discreetly hidden from view of the farmer's wife.

'Good morning, Mrs Barstow—how very kind,' Alan

managed to say, and Claire felt helpless with love and admiration of his sexy, husky voice in calm command of the situation.

'Plenty of hot water for baths or showers, whichever you like, Dr Jarvis,' and Mrs Barstow retreated after putting the tray down on the bedside table nearest to Alan.

Claire heard the door close and wished they could resume where they had left off, but she knew that she was torturing herself with an impossible dream.

Alan clinked the side of a cup with a spoon then ran the spoon down her bare back.

'Tea,' he said. 'This is where we came in, I believe.'

Claire couldn't bring herself to emerge from her hideaway, however much Alan insisted on teasing the upper half of her spine which was visible, and after a moment or two of receiving no response he bent over her and pulled her into his arms.

'Darling, I'm sorry, but I guess we'd better——' He shrugged, and then gently matched his lips to hers in a powerful kiss that sealed the end of everything. 'I'll take a rain check on the continuation,' he whispered. 'There'll be other Sundays when you can spoil me.'

Claire could have wept with disappointment. Her eyes were moist as she clung to him. How she wanted him, needed him; her body and emotions were keyed up with suspense but Alan only indulged in some playful frolic before finally breaking away from her and pouring out the tea.

Through her liquid gaze she regarded his masculine back, appreciating the youthful magnificence of him, and she had to fight back the tears and the urge to hug him desperately.

'Come on then, lazybones, sit up,' he ordered, and as she did so he put his arm round her, one hand gently supporting her breast, the other fondling her until she was forced to smile up at him, resting her head against his shoulder. He passed her a cup of tea and she wished, oh, how she wished that time would freeze.

Alan drank his tea left-handed, despite Claire's warning that he might spill it.

'Then it would be Mrs Barstow's fault for spoiling us,' he said light-heartedly. He kept Claire in his embrace until the tea was gone. The silence was tense yet magical, and neither spoke again until Alan asked: 'How does the leg feel today?'

'Not too bad,' Claire replied softly, not wishing to spoil their togetherness.

When Alan had replaced the cups and saucers on the tray he pushed back all the bedclothes and took a look at Claire's leg.

She felt a moment's embarrassment but somehow now modesty seemed irrelevant.

'When we reach Birchdale I'll see to it properly and give you an anti-tetanus injection,' Alan said. 'At least the blood hasn't seeped through the dressing overnight. Now—I'll have a shower while you have a wash here. I expect you'd rather soak in your own bath at home.'

Claire agreed and although neither of them voiced their reluctance to rise and face the day, there was a mutual feeling of having been cheated of something promising.

Mrs Barstow had prepared a huge breakfast.

'How are the jeans, Mrs Jarvis?' she asked as they entered the big farmhouse dining room.

Claire started awkwardly, and Alan rose to the occasion in his own inimitable way.

'I've advised my wife against wearing those ridiculous tight jeans,' he said in a jovial voice, but with a dark warning glance directed towards Claire. 'Not at all suitable for this type of countryside.'

'I find jeans comfortable for walking,' Claire answered

back, then with a generous smile at Mrs Barstow added: 'It was very kind of you to mend them, and I see you managed to sponge the blood off.'

'Yes, my dear—it was no trouble—better to do it while it was fresh, if you know what I mean.' She laughed boisterously. 'They've been hung by the boiler all night, so are quite dry.'

'I'm sorry to have put you to so much trouble.'

'It was my pleasure, Mrs Jarvis; now eat a good breakfast or I shall think there's something wrong with my cooking.'

'Just as well my wife put her jeans on before breakfast or she'd never get into them,' Alan said, and Claire decided it best to enter into the spirit of the charade with enthusiasm.

'They're not *that* tight—*darling*.'

Alan needed no encouragement. From the opposite side of the small table he mouthed a kiss and then caught the farmer's wife's eye with a wink.

'Excuse us, Mrs Barstow, but we haven't been married long.'

Claire wanted to giggle, and wondered whether she shouldn't put the great man down with a remark like: 'No, just last last night actually for your benefit,' but Mrs Barstow was the one to spring the surprise.

'You're a Sister at Moorlands, aren't you?' she asked.

Claire felt the blood ooze from her cheeks.

'Yes, that's right,' she admitted.

'My young Donald tried to cut his foot off a year or so ago in some of the machinery. They did wonders for him at Moorlands. That young Dr Boyd—he's a nice lad. I thought I recognised you—are you still there?'

'Nurses don't give in easily,' Alan answered on her behalf, 'and of course she still uses her maiden name.'

'A very worthy profession, but you'll have to give it up when the little ones start to come.'

This was going a little too far, Claire thought, but let him wriggle out of that one!

'And that can't be too soon for me,' Alan told Mrs Barstow readily. 'Nice to have a little time to ourselves though while we get Birchdale up to scratch. Needs quite a bit doing to it, and that all costs money.'

'You're young, plenty of time. I'll just go and do some toast.' She hurried away to the kitchen, and as Claire emptied her plate of bacon, eggs, sausages and tomatoes she glanced at Alan, who was studying her seriously.

'May I compliment you on your performance,' he said in a low voice. 'You should have been an actress.'

'You didn't do so badly yourself,' then with a giggle Claire added: 'You're a devious liar—*darling*—I shall never be able to trust you.'

Mrs Barstow returned with toast, and Claire poured more coffee while the conversation turned to the school bus, whose running times were somewhat irregular, so there seemed to be an element of hurry in their final departure.

Claire returned to the bedroom while Alan settled up with Mrs Barstow. She fixed her rucksack on her back and stood looking out of the window. There was no mist this morning, but it was dull and Finchfigg looming in the distance didn't look at all inviting. She turned back to the interior of the room. It was all so cosy, so intimate, and she knew she would cherish the memory of last night and this morning with a special kind of love. She didn't hear Alan come in until he squeezed her hand.

'It wasn't all bad was it, Claire?' he asked as if wanting to know her true feelings.

Claire raised her eyebrows, deciding to be daring enough to tell him that she wouldn't have missed it for anything, but Mrs Barstow's voice called from below: 'It's coming down the hill, sir,' and Alan picked up his rucksack and led Claire hurriedly down the stairs.

The bus pulled up in the lane and they joined the load of children, some excited and noisy, others thoughtful with an apparent dread of Monday morning at school. Twenty minutes later it stopped outside the village school and Alan and Claire set off through the quaint village on foot, past the church next to the school with its solid square tower and handsome clock. The post office and general store was already busy with customers, and at the end of the village they had to wait while the farmer shepherded his flock of sheep over the narrow stone bridge on their way from the sheep-dip.

Claire always found country routine fascinating, and when a young lamb jumped clear over some of the others she looked up at Alan and the glance which passed between them expressed their amusement with warmth. He squeezed her hand again; it was becoming a habit, Claire thought, and one which they must break before reaching his home.

Birchdale was distinctive by its elegance. A characteristic manor type house built of stone, and standing in several acres of rural grounds. A gravel path wound through parkland of birches and rowans, oak, ash and sycamore to the huge front door, which stood open.

There were signs that structural renovation and alterations had been made recently, and when Alan showed Claire into the superb entrance hall she could see at a glance that he valued this ancestral home. He opened a door to the right of the semi-spiral staircase which was a tasteful feature in natural oak wood, into a spacious lounge.

Claire was shocked and Alan's brows puckered in an angry frown at the sight of the mess everywhere. Bottles and glasses were strewn on every available surface, with paper serviettes scattered all over the floor.

'I must apologise for this,' he said shortly. 'I'll see if I can rustle up some coffee before I look at your leg.'

'Alan, there's no need, honestly. I am a nurse. I'm quite capable of cleaning it and making sure it's okay.'

'*I* want to see it, and an anti-tetanus injection is a must, as you haven't had one during the past three years.'

He went away and Claire heard him conversing with a woman, then he ran up the staircase two steps at a time. Some minutes later Claire shuddered at the heated exchange which echoed down to every corner of the old house. She felt embarrassed and it immediately turned their night of bliss to a fading memory of illicit intrigue. Even though it had not been planned Claire realised that if she were in Fiona's shoes she, too, would be pretty upset.

She had time to glance around the room. The furnishings were in brown and gold, rich and regal-looking, with a carpet of the same colouring but with a touch of red added. Heavy drapes in brown velvet hung at the huge bay windows, also at the french doors which opened out to a pathway with lush green lawns beyond. Alan fitted in well in such a background, Claire thought, but Fiona? She was a model specimen of modern tastes and fashion— a mite too modern perhaps for Birchdale. Modern with riotous living habits as well, Claire noticed by the state of the room which had obviously angered Alan. Some party there must have been. Who could blame Fiona, if she had been left to her own devices while Alan spent the day enjoying his freedom? Claire felt guilty, but irritated with Alan who was, after all, only making a convenience of her.

Why should a married man with such a beautiful wife want to make love to another woman? It wasn't as if they had enjoyed a long-standing working relationship, so that finding themselves alone together would lead to the inevitable. That might have been excusable, Claire decided, but no allowances could be made for the cold-blooded way Alan Jarvis seemed to prefer to go his own way, and repeatedly make passes at Claire. The fact that she loved him meant that she wanted to find the best in him, and looking again at the untidy remnants of a drinking party she had to admit that maybe he had something to put up with which drove him to going on long walks and visiting the hospital at weekends.

Claire's mind flew back to Moorlands. She couldn't wait to get back there. There would be Richard waiting hopefully, and Claire felt an upsurge of warmth for him. There were the Wilsons too—would Mrs Wilson have regained consciousness? and dear Mr Whitmarsh, as well as the group of younger men who tended to pal up and stick together, all conspiring to make life as difficult as possible for the nursing staff with their practical jokes and teasing.

No way did Claire intend to be 'the other woman'. Alan Jarvis had proved to her that he could make her happy, but just as the stars predicted, he was ineligible, and that must bring an end to their relationship, and any beautiful daydreams that Claire had woven into her thoughts. Through her thoughts she was trying to shut out the raised voices which still persisted—getting louder now as Alan came down the stairs.

'Take it to my surgery, Mrs Atkinson, please.' He entered the room in a rush, then with a bad-tempered sigh and a look of fury beckoned to Claire.

'Come on, let's see if you're fit to work.'

Claire got up from the chair which should have offered luxurious comfort but didn't, and followed him out into the hall again.

There were so many things to say, but she knew this was not the right time and place. In just a few moments a tense feeling had sprung up between them, and they had become two professional people again.

Alan led the way briskly to another room across the hall, a good-sized room which had been fitted out and equipped as a surgery where he could see private patients.

The housekeeper had placed the tray with china cups and saucers, and coffee pot to match, on his elegant desk, and he motioned Claire to take the chair on the opposite side to him. Then she didn't feel professional at all, but as if she had come for an interview.

Claire never knew how she got through the next half-hour. They were just finishing coffee, neither of them daring to speak, when a young woman came into the room. She was wearing a white overall and almost nothing else, so that her slender figure moved sensuously beneath it.

'Fiona, this is my nursing sister at the hospital, Claire Tyndall,' Alan introduced abruptly.

Claire managed to mumble the appropriate greeting to Fiona who looked as white as her overall, especially in contrast to her lustrous raven-coloured hair. Her eyes were hidden behind a huge pair of tinted glasses, and she nodded in response to Claire's acknowledgment.

If Claire hadn't known it was the same person whom she had seen driving the Granada—was it her's or Alan's?—she would never have recognised Fiona, who walked gracefully across the room to a cupboard.

'Go behind the screen and slip off your jeans, please, then lie on the couch,' Alan commanded.

Meekly Claire did as she was told, but inwardly felt indignant that she was being treated like one of his patients. It was all too cold and clinical now, and her one thought was to get away.

Fiona silently did her master's bidding, preparing the anti-tetanus injection and a special dressing for Claire's leg which, in spite of Claire's insistence that it was all right, throbbed quite painfully at times.

Icy displeasure hung between Fiona and Alan while Claire tried not to show her sensitivity to the situation, and when her leg was rebandaged she slipped off the couch, meaning to leave at once.

Alan washed his hands at a corner washbasin.

'It's nice and clean, Claire,' he informed her, 'but I think it might be a good idea to keep off it for a day or two. I expect you could do with a couple of extra days off.'

'I'd rather return to duty—sir,' she replied obstinately. 'After all it's only a flesh wound.'

He smiled, but it accompanied a sarcastic glance at her formality.

'Just as well you had a decent amount of flesh in that particular part of you. I'll go and get the car out to run you to Lakeside.'

She should have protested, but changed her mind as he hurried out of a back door, and when Claire heard the car engine start up she picked up her rucksack from the hall and then returned to the surgery door.

'I'm sorry to have intruded, Mrs Jarvis, thanks for your help.'

The dark-haired woman turned from the desk and stared, then lowered her spectacles an inch or so and peered over the top at Claire. She didn't speak, just pursed her lips and nodded, and raised one hand in a semi-circular wave. The suspicion of a smile briefly showed on her otherwise colourless expression, and Claire left the house in a hurry.

She sat beside Alan, not wanting to talk, but hating the insoluble gulf that widened between them. Like a piece of elastic when stretched to the limit, it would have to snap. She tried to tell herself *I will not love this man*, but she knew that it was a useless warning. She loved him, hated him, pitied him. That was the worst part. Pitying him for the type of woman he had chosen for a wife, wishing desperately that she could take her place, knowing how much she would worship him and take a pride in his beautiful home, Birchdale.

Some people just didn't know when they were well off, Claire thought, disgusted by the superior lounge being cheapened by the filthy remains of a questionable party. But, she supposed, Alan only had himself to blame. Claire was mystified. Fiona was apparently a qualified nurse, yet hadn't he mentioned something about a 'dreary theatre party' the previous Sunday?

Claire was thankful to see her Fiesta still standing in the car-park at Lakeside. Alan drew in beside it and Claire jumped out instantly, going to the rear boot to get her rucksack.

Alan put his hand on the strap then looked intently at Claire before letting her take it.

'You're back in one piece, Claire, but I still think a couple of days' rest wouldn't do you any harm.'

'I'm fine—and—thanks,' she added in a croaky whisper.

'It wasn't all bad, was it?' he said again for the umpteenth time, then with an impatient sigh he banged his hand on the edge of the car boot.

'What can I say, Claire? Fiona is——' He couldn't find the right words, so Claire averted the awkward moment by taking her rucksack from him.

'Thanks, Alan—be seeing you,' and she walked over to her own car. She had unlocked it and put the rucksack on her passenger seat before she heard the slam of Alan's boot, and as she started up and reversed she noticed that he was still motionless beside the Granada.

She gave a hoot on her car horn, courageously showing that she didn't care a jot about him, or Fiona, but her spirits were low by the time she reached her flat.

There wasn't too much time to allow herself to moon over the past twenty-four hours, and it wasn't until she was walking through the corridor at Moorlands towards the Orthopaedic unit that she realised that some difficult questions might be asked.

The Senior Nursing Officer was the first person Claire encountered, who met her with concern over her little accident. No matter how casual Claire tried to be, she couldn't help wondering just how much Alan Jarvis had revealed.

When she reached her unit it was evident that her sister-colleagues in the unit also knew, and had been requested to share the work load so that Claire could rest her leg as much as possible. She spent much of the afternoon studying the previous day's reports and at around tea-time was about to visit each patient when Mike Boyd breezed into her office.

'Hullo, gorgeous,' he greeted. 'How are things? Hear you had a rough night.'

Claire felt her cheeks tighten. Mike was the sort who would want a blow by blow account.

'I'm okay,' she answered non-committally, 'but what happened to the rest of you?'

'Oh, haven't you heard yet? The mini-bus which was to have taken us as far as Lakeside refused to start. Being Sunday, we couldn't get a mechanic very quickly, and then of course we were doubtful with the mist so by the time we reached Lakeside on foot it was lunch-time, and you'd got most of the food. I must say I was surprised you set out on your own, Claire.'

'Mr Jarvis seemed to think it offered a challenge, and in the event it turned out to be a lovely afternoon.'

'Some creep you turned out to be—making up to the boss and going off together,' Mike taunted.

'*You* let *me* down,' Claire retorted hotly.

'We did try to catch up with you, but you know how it is once a party of ten or twelve reach a pub, and Jo Morrison does an excellent Ploughman's, so we just did a short walk and back to Moorlands. I hear you hurt yourself?'

'Climbing over a wall. Caught my jeans on some

barbed wire—it's nothing, really.'

'Alan seemed to think you should have gone sick.'

'I can catch up on some paperwork—just to rest my leg for a day or two. It's nothing, Mike, honestly,' she repeated.

Mike shrugged. 'If you say so. Your flock will all be delighted to see you back.'

'Nothing much new happening here,' Claire said, wanting to turn the conversation to something other than the fell walk.

'A couple of accident cases in I.T.U., and you've got a distressed pot-holer with a broken leg and collar bone.'

'Mrs Wilson still the same?' Claire queried.

'Yes, but a stronger, steadier pulse—we're still hopeful. Glad to say Debbie's quietened down a lot, and her father is making great strides. Determined to pull through for Debbie's sake, in case his wife doesn't.'

Mike discussed a few of the other patients, in particular those who were to be on Alan's theatre list the following day, and then departed.

Claire visited each ward, making light of her minor injury and being vague about what had occurred despite the constant enquiries from staff and patients alike, and she was glad of the excuse to return and remain in her office. She stirred her tea thoughtfully. Richard Lynch had only just got back from the swimming pool when she had reached his ward. It had given her a real boost to see his dark eyes light up even though they were not able to have a private conversation. He was walking with two sticks quite confidently, and Claire knew that he soon had to face his future. Here was a man who was fond of her for her own sake. Even though he had no one else, and that being the reason he had turned to Claire, she felt that his feelings for her were quite genuine. She was deeply attracted by his handsome good looks and warmth.

Would she ever learn to love him with the same passion that she felt for Alan? The kind of passion that made her unmindful of the fact that he too was a married man—perhaps unhappily, so that he was looking for a side interest? Somehow she knew that she had to check her feelings for Alan before they were allowed to dominate her life. He was playing a game with her and she hoped any sign of affection she had shown him would be viewed in the same light. He had warned her of becoming involved with Richard, but she saw that as a way to prevent herself from becoming involved with Alan.

She refused to be made a fool of. Whatever his marital problems were he must sort them out without using her. Perhaps he and Fiona were unsuited, and Claire felt a moment of sympathy for him if he were tied to a woman he did not love. But she mustn't let her love for him blind her to his faults. He had cheated and lied at Mrs Barstow's, Claire remembered. Supposing Mrs Barstow ever met the real Mrs Jarvis, or had occasion to visit the hospital? Claire felt herself go cold at the prospect of such a situation. From now on she and the consultant surgeon of Moorlands were merely colleagues. . . .

The day had started off well, but by the time Claire went off duty it had turned cloudy and dull. When she came to the wooden bench in the shrubbery she found Richard patiently waiting there. He didn't get up but patted the place beside him, and she sat down eagerly.

Immediately Richard took her into his arms and kissed her long and arduously.

'I've missed you, darling,' he said, 'and what I want to do can best be done sitting down.' He took off her cap and allowed his hand to explore beneath her cape as he covered her face with kisses.

'What's the matter, Claire? You've cooled,' he said.

'Not here,' she said, 'we might be seen.'

'So when and where? When can I get out of this prison for a weekend?'

'You'll have to ask Mr Jarvis.'

'Did you find a place for us to stay?'

'No. There are plenty of places though—hotels, guest houses.'

'Together, Claire—I want us to be alone together with no interruptions, no inhibitions.'

'Don't rush me, Richard, there's plenty of time.'

He kissed her again, gently at first but then with a fierceness that demanded response. She wanted to kiss him back, but her thoughts would keep returning to the bedroom at the farm and when she opened her eyes she knew that in the wrong man's arms her lips would remain impassive. But Richard was a determined man. Not only in persevering with his ability to walk again, but to woo Claire. Every evening he met her in the shrubbery, and every night Claire forced herself to believe that she loved him.

Alan Jarvis seemed to be avoiding her, which helped Claire to forget him. When he did visit the wards under her supervision, apart from enquiring after her injury, which was healing rapidly, his attention was exclusively given to his patients, and Claire suspected that he felt ashamed now at his illicit night with her. She tried to forget it, tried to pretend that it had never happened, but the awakening of her love for Alan which had become apparent during that night stuck firmly in her mind, and seemed to come between herself and Richard. She lay awake at night wondering how she could overcome this desperate longing for a man who was, as her stars predicted, ineligible.

The solution had to be with Richard. As the days passed by she deliberately set out to react to his charm, convinced that if Alan realised there was something between her and Richard he would believe that Claire felt nothing for him. She didn't intend to be second best, and Richard, though he still refused to discuss the past, claimed that he had no other loves beside Claire.

One morning when the consultant did his round, looking distinguished in his dark suit, his velvety eyes calmer than of late and affording Claire a hint of the old magic which made her heart beat faster, he came to Richard's bed and spent longer than usual discussing his progress. After Richard had shown off his expertise by walking smartly down the ward with the aid of his sticks and returning hesitantly but proudly without them, Alan clapped him on the back enthusiastically.

'Well done, Mr Lynch. Your determination has paid off.' He sighed. 'Of course in the normal way, if you lived within easy reach of Moorlands, we should be sending you home for a few days.'

'I'm ready to go out into the big outside world for a weekend, Mr Jarvis,' Richard said confidently.

Alan looked suspicious. 'You have friends, or somewhere to go?'

Richard shot a glance in Claire's direction before saying: 'I was going to an hotel or guest house. I need to make contact again with people, and start to explore the business world—but—I may very well go to stay with a friend.'

'Not too far away?' Alan queried.

'Quite close, in fact—but we may decide to go deeper into the Lake district. We'll see what the weather does by the weekend.'

'You realise we must have an address, a telephone number? It would be much easier all round if you had some family in this country,' Alan added.

Richard's black eyes met and held Alan's inquisitive ones, warning him against further probing.

'I have no family, Mr Jarvis, but I am fortunate in having a good friend. I'll see that Sister Tyndall has a telephone number.'

Richard caught Claire's eye brazenly, and she knew that he meant to go through with this proposed weekend together, and that he had invited himself to her flat.

She hoped her pink cheeks did not convey the guilt she experienced at such a thought. But as the day progressed the idea appealed to her more. It would be good for Richard to get away from the hospital atmosphere, and it would be a pleasure for her to have company for the five days due to her, also convenient for Richard that her flat was situated on the ground floor.

When she was finishing the report that evening Richard came to her in the office.

'Well,' he said smugly, 'do you approve of my plan?'

'You've dropped me right in it, haven't you?' she replied with a grin. 'But my flat is comfortable and large enough for two.'

'You're not angry with me, darling?'

'Of course not, Richard, but it won't be easy to arrange.'

'You can tell me to go to hell if you don't want me. I hadn't schemed to use you—it just presented itself while I was talking to the great man.'

'How can we keep it a secret?'

'I'll go to an hotel for the first day, somewhere with a ground floor room or lift, then come on to you on Friday morning—unless you'd like to join me at the hotel? My firm have been very generous after all—they've also offered me another post at the same level, but in Scotland. That's between you and me for the moment. I'm not in a hurry to leave Moorlands—not while there's you, darling.'

'Scotland isn't too far away, Richard, and I'm glad you've got a job fixed up.'

'It's all right, then, for the weekend?—you are off, aren't you?'

She nodded, recognising in his bright, dangerous eyes that she was desperately needed. She only hoped she could fulfil such an obligation, knowing that it was Alan she really loved.

CHAPTER NINE

CLAIRE's feelings were mixed as she cleaned her flat in readiness for Richard's arrival. She packed up all her winter's activities tools, and hung the latest painting of which she felt modestly proud in the spare bedroom above the end of the bed. Richard could lie and study it, she thought with a smirk, and as quickly dismissed that proposition. She felt quite certain that Richard would have another one, a proposition which, while not quite as binding as she hoped for, would be imaginative, and help her to put Alan right out of her mind for good.

That, she realised, would be difficult so long as they worked together, but if Richard was going to work in Scotland, why shouldn't she make a move too? She had not planned such a dramatic change in her life, she would miss her friends, Mike and Miriam—no doubt they would come up with all sorts of reasons why she shouldn't take such a drastic step. But they didn't know what sort of a future Richard could offer Claire.

She sat down heavily on the side of the bed she had just made up with loving care for Richard. Neither did *she* know what Richard had to offer! A sordid affair? Living together wasn't what she wanted, but then she couldn't have what she wanted so why throw away all chances of happiness?

It was June now, and after a bad start with wet and dismal weather, hot, sunny days were forecast for the remainder of the month, and when Richard telephoned from his hotel on Friday morning it was already warm and summery.

All the arrangements had been made with the utmost secrecy, and the hotel's telephone number duly noted in

Richard's folder before Claire started her short holiday on the Thursday. At first Richard had elected to travel everywhere by taxi, but Claire offered to save him some expense by going to fetch him from the hotel. She ran up the steps to the hotel reception feeling quite light-headed, and Richard, anxiously awaiting her in the entrance lounge showed his approval of her blue floral dress and white sandals.

'Darling,' he greeted with a hug and kiss, 'you look lovely, just like summer itself.' Then as they followed the porter carrying Richard's bag down to the car, he whispered, 'I've given them your telephone number in case of anyone wanting to catch up with me. There isn't anyone, of course, unless one of your colleagues gets suspicious. The hotel people think I'm a rep, so now all we have to do is enjoy ourselves.'

Claire joined in the surreptitious game with a zest she hadn't expected. But, she argued mentally, if Alan Jarvis could play games so could she. Behind the wheel of her Fiesta she drove carefully, realising that Richard might be nervous after his accident, and she wore dark sunglasses hoping that she was suitably disguised should they meet any of the hospital's staff. But that was unlikely, as Richard had deliberately chosen an hotel on the same side of the town as Claire's flat.

Claire suspected that there were a few prying eyes from adjacent flats as she drew up to the front door and helped Richard out, and as soon as they were inside behind closed doors Claire switched the kettle on.

'A pleasant flat—much larger than I expected,' Richard said, taking stock of his surroundings.

'Only the basic rooms, but they're all a decent size. Come through to the spare room. You can leave all your stuff here.' Suddenly she was overcome by embarrassment. She might just as well have said: 'I don't have any spare room in my wardrobe and cupboards, but my bed will be adequate for the two of us.' Colour flooded her cheeks as she hurried through the hallway into the single room with Richard's bag. She succeeded in composing herself a little by the time he caught up with her.

'I do a fair bit of sketching and painting,' she explained. 'It's my hobby, but I've packed it all up to make room for you. I hope this will suit?'

His dark eyes gazed at her fondly, and Claire knew that he could read every thought in her head. He held open his arms and as Claire fell into them he all but lost his balance. They laughed together as Richard clung to Claire for support.

'I'm not too steady yet, Claire. I hope my performance in other feats will be more polished, but—it's a long time—I hope you'll be patient with me.'

'Let's just take things as they come, Richard,' Claire whispered. 'I'll make some coffee. It's such a gorgeous morning, shall we have it in the garden?'

She showed him into the elegant lounge and took him out on to the patio. When she joined him with coffee and Black Forest gâteaux later, he smiled appreciatively and held out his hand to her.

'This is how home should be,' he said gratefully. 'I see you're going to spoil me beautifully.'

'You've been outrageously spoilt for the past two months, Richard,' she said in mock reproach.

'And I've loved every minute of it, darling.' He ruffled her silky blonde hair and let his hand slide provocatively down her back, and with each minute any strain Claire had felt at first just ebbed away. Richard was good company, and she found it easy to relax with him. She had cooked and prepared delicacies in her usual enthusiastic way, being domestic the way she so often dreamed of being with a man who expressed his delight at her efforts.

They talked at length about her art work, Richard proving himself to be a connoisseur of the arts in general.

He appreciated good music, contributed to his firm's house magazine with humorous anecdotes as well as strip cartoons, and after lunch they spread out a rug on the lawn to enjoy the sun, while Claire settled herself comfortably with her sketchpad on her knee.

Richard watched for a while then he said: 'Go and get your bikini on, darling, and give me the sketchpad.'

'As long as you promise to destroy whatever you draw of me,' she said, tossing back her hair and running in through the lounge.

Richard whistled softly when Claire reappeared, and his ebony eyes appraised her slim form, the milk-white skin, smooth and supple, shown off to advantage almost in its entirety.

'Don't stare,' Claire admonished mischievously, 'it's rude.'

Richard laughed boyishly. 'I was just going to ask, why bother?'

Claire hit the top of his head with the sketchpad. 'I thought you'd like your money's worth,' she said.

He ran his fingers up the expanse of one of her legs, hovering over the spot where a jagged scar was still visible.

'That was nasty,' he said, and Claire willed away the reminder of Alan and how it had come about.

'You're tiny,' Richard observed, 'but wiry, a really splendid figure in fact.'

'You're a connoisseur in models as well?' she asked impishly. 'I eat too much.'

'But you work it all off, darling, your job keeps you trim.'

Claire dropped down on to the rug beside him and he glanced round at the nearby flats before he kissed her gently.

'I love you,' he said suddenly, 'but you're much too sweet and lovely for me.'

'Now you've spoilt it,' Claire answered with a pout, but she didn't let it mask her vivaciousness. She was happy, enjoying a cosiness which she found extremely satisfying.

'I don't want you to sit here, Claire.' Richard pointed to a corner of the lawn. 'Apart from being a wicked temptation, I can't sketch you this close. Drape yourself around that rose bush, or better still by that cherub or whatever monstrosity you've got there.'

'That's my own personal Eros,' she said, 'God of love. I bought him from the jumble stall at Moorlands Open Day last year.'

'We'll put you together and see what comes out. Without the apology for a bikini would be better, of course, but we hadn't better shock the neighbours.'

Claire sat beside the small statue, her knees drawn up to her chin as she laughed across at Richard.

'Darling, that's awful,' he said. 'I don't mean you are—any pose suits me, but let's be a little artistic. Could you—would you mind going topless?' he suggested hesitantly.

Claire pursed her lips thoughtfully.

'Go on,' Richard urged. 'I'm sure you're the expert in being provocative.'

'Not in this particular spot,' she said wistfully. 'If I can go over on the patio it might be better.'

She slipped inside the lounge and took off her bra-top. The briefs were only minute with a shoe-lace cord at her thighs, and the pose in which Richard set her up allowed him to delete the briefs in his sketch.

'I wish I could draw you,' she said as she sat quite still on the log, 'but I'm not very good with portraits.'

'It's what I do best,' Richard said. 'Especially delectable girls with the right attributes. You should try going around naked more often, Claire.'

'You're making me blush,' she quipped.

'Sorry, darling,' and he pursed his lips in a mock kiss. He sketched her in several poses, the last one lying on her stomach on the grass, one leg raised from the knee, her chin propped up on her hands. When he'd finished she had to agree that he was very talented, but when she attempted to sketch him it ended in high-spirited frolic.

Richard was fun, seemingly having shed ten years while in the company of Claire, and when she taunted him skittishly he chased her into the flat. When he didn't follow her to the bedroom she went back to look for him always fearing that he might have fallen, but he was lurking behind the lounge door and pounced on her as she entered the room.

She linked her arms around his neck, knowing that the sight of her cool, naked slimness was arousing his desire. Above all she wanted to please him, but as he caressed her, tantalising her senses, she closed her eyes and imagined she was in Alan's arms.

Richard was tender in his loving and soothed her, but his gentleness lacked the excitement which Alan's touch could arouse in her. However much they kissed and allowed passion to rule their heads, Claire knew that her heart was elsewhere. Finally Richard pushed her hands away, running his fingertips down her bare arms until she wriggled sensuously.

'Shameless hussy,' he reproached jovially. 'We'd better cool off, it's too early for that.'

Claire laughingly escaped his clutches and went to her bedroom to dress. It was several minutes before she was aware of him standing in the doorway watching her.

'Is there anywhere you'd like to go, or anything you'd like to do?' Claire asked shyly.

Richard raised his eyebrows before dropping his gaze to her bed briefly, then with a clear, honest look he said simply: 'We'll get one thing sorted out, darling. I came here to be with you because I've come to love you,

Claire—but, because I love you so much I refuse to ruin your life.'

'Richard,' Claire managed in a surprised voice and taking a step forward.

He held up a warning hand. 'Before we get carried away, or let our emotions take over, I insist on taking up your offer of the spare bed.' His intense black eyes met her blue ones levelly.

'If that's what you want, Richard,' Claire said meekly.

'It's not what I want, darling. I want *you*—desperately—and we've created a tempting and difficult situation. I've spoilt other people's lives, Claire, messed up my own by my selfishness, but I will not upset yours. There can never be anything for keeps between us, Claire, so let's be happy together—just for a little while, and enjoy a weekend of fun.'

'Oh, Richard.' Suddenly Claire was weeping as she fell into his arms. Arms that held her tenderly, gently comforting, even protective, and as she hid her face in his shoulder she knew that she was crying with relief.

It was no good pretending any more. It was Alan she loved and Alan who would dominate her thoughts, even though she couldn't have him. She thought she could have been content to share Richard's life, hoping that in time he would teach her to love him as he claimed he loved her. But did he? If that was true then he wouldn't allow anything to come between them, and something did. But what was it?

They settled for a quiet evening watching television and eating. Claire could hardly believe the happy contentment that continued to exist between them. It seemed an incredible situation, yet it worked, and if this was the way Richard wanted it Claire was pleased to accept his terms. Friendship that started out this way often came to mean much more than a love-at-first-sight relationship.

They planned eagerly for the following day.

'What had you in mind?' Richard asked running his fingers idly through her hair as they sat cuddled together on the settee.

'If it's going to be another lovely day, how about going to Windermere? A trip on one of the boats, dinner at an hotel before we come home?'

'That sounds lovely, darling, especially when you say "come home" like that and I know it includes me—but don't let it fool you. I meant what I said, my dear.'

She reached up and kissed him lightly on his lips.

'Nothing's going to spoil your weekend out of Moorlands, Richard darling. One day at a time—remember?' she reminded him.

They set off early next morning and eagerly, stopping off in the first small town to visit a men's outfitters where Richard bought a whole new rig-out.

'A suit can wait,' he told the assistant. 'A casual jacket, two pairs of slacks, shirts, socks and underwear will see me through the next couple of months.'

They left the shop an hour later, Richard looking smart but holidayish in lightweight natural coloured trousers, a turquoise blue shirt and a thick fair-isle sweater. The rest of his purchases were boxed and lay in the rear of Claire's car.

En route they stopped for coffee at a small country pub before travelling the rest of the way to Windermere, where they pulled in by the lakeside to eat the lunch Claire had prepared. It was a perfect day for a boat-ride across the calm blue water. Claire had come suitably dressed in an apple-green trouser suit, the top of which was pleated from a yoke edged with white saddle-stitch, and the short sleeves were similarly designed. Richard watched and openly admired her constantly and Claire, who had visited Windermere many times before, enjoyed pointing out landmarks and the scenic beauty which they passed.

Back at the pier they took their time, allowing others to disembark before them, as Richard was slow and still had difficulty in negotiating steps and awkward levels. A queue of people were waiting on the pier for the next trip, and as Claire held Richard's arm her gaze was attracted to someone standing in the queue.

She was grateful for the support of Richard's masculine strength as Alan Jarvis met her glance with cold disapproval. He nodded, and Claire returned the half-hearted greeting with a weak smile, thankful that her attention was drawn back to Richard at that moment as he stumbled on an uneven board on the pier.

But inwardly her reactions were violent. The swift realisation that he was so close, looking immaculate as always in light blue slacks and a navy blue blazer, tore at her heartstrings, causing the adrenalin to flow erratically. Her glimpse may have been brief, but it allowed her time to absorb the lovely Fiona by his side, clutching at his arm and looking as fashionable as ever in a white linen suit and a nautical-type scarf covering her hair. Claire couldn't be sure whether she had noticed her or not from behind the large, tinted glasses.

'Is something wrong?' Richard's voice was full of concern, and Claire knew she could not disguise the way her emotions had been taunted.

'Didn't you see him?' Her vivacious laugh was not particularly convincing.

'Who?'

'Don't turn round—Mr Jarvis and his wife are standing in the queue.'

Richard made no attempt to verify her statement. Instead his equable scrutiny conveyed his sympathy. Claire felt the slightest squeeze of pressure from his fingers on her hand.

'Seeing him with his wife bothers you?' It wasn't a question, not one he expected her to answer but a way of expressing his understanding.

'Seeing him at all on my day off bothers me.' Claire tried to sound vindictive, which made Richard laugh.

'I'd willingly change places with him if I could,' he said.

'You mean you fancy his wife?' Claire asked.

'I didn't see her, but I'm sure I could put up with her just to make it easy for you to have a day with him.'

'What makes you think I want a day with *him*?' Claire retorted indignantly, her senses returning to a more normal balance.

Richard just laughed, but caught her in a wild embrace and kissed her cheek lightly. Claire felt embarrassed. Was Alan watching? What did it matter if he was? she thought, her heart plummetting to the depths of despair. He had Fiona!

They crossed the road and found a small, cosy tea-shop where they enjoyed tea, and scones with jam and cream and afterwards they returned to the car. Claire's attention was drawn at once to the smart Granada parked in a bay a few hundred yards from Claire's in the huge car-park, and she was glad to be leaving Windermere. They travelled in comparative silence for some distance before Claire managed to recompose herself. This was Richard's weekend; he had said he loved her even though there could never be anything lasting between them. So she resolved not to let Alan Jarvis spoil anything for him.

They drove through some of the most picturesque and captivating scenery to be found in Great Britain. The wild recklessness of it in winter, the pure inspiration of rural nature in its prime, never failed to fill Claire with joy, and a peace which embalmed her anxiety as it did now. Richard had a calming effect on her too. He seemed to understand when she needed quiet, and when to enthuse with her in the beauty of the countryside. On the homeward route they stopped many times to just sit and admire the wonders of the universe, and during one of the pauses they decided to go home to freshen up before going to an hotel for dinner, but once they got to Claire's flat she realised that Richard was tired. It had been a full day, even if he had only been sitting beside her as they travelled.

'Shall we call it a day, Richard?' she asked hesitantly.

He gave her a wistful glance and smiled apologetically.

'I'm sorry, darling—I've loved every minute of being with you, and I'll get ready and take you out to dinner rather than spoil your day.'

'There's tomorrow,' she said. 'I've nothing planned. It's been hot and tiring and I think you've done enough for one day.'

'Then tomorrow it is.' He took the flask and empty food boxes from her and gave her a big bear-like hug.

'You're a wonderful girl, Claire. I wish I was in a position to do things so differently, but, if you only knew the pleasure I get from being with you here, the nearest thing I've had to home for a very long time.'

'It's nice for me to have someone to share it with,' she said fondly, and held her mouth up to his for a kiss.

Later, while Claire prepared salmon salad, Richard had a bath, and after they had eaten they watched television, but Richard fell asleep so Claire persuaded him to go to bed early. She was glad of the chance of an early night herself, but she didn't sleep immediately. Instead she lay wide-eyed and thoughtful, staring at the stars visible through the window, and wondered what cruel twist of fate—or was it the position of the stars?—that made her love a man who could never be anything to her. And what right had Alan Jarvis to condemn her for offering friendship to Richard? Who was he to condemn anyone? she thought angrily. He had loved her, shared her bed, which had been unforgivable when all the time he already had a wife!

She had thought sharing Richard's weekend would have helped her to get over Alan but she was glad Richard hadn't made any demands even though he admitted to wanting her so passionately. She would never get over Alan Jarvis. She hated, yet loved the way his discerning eyes could strip her of every ounce of self-control. They had become so close during that fell-walk, close in agreeable companionship in much the same way as she was with Richard, yet with Alan she had felt as if she were in the wake of some impending exciting eruption, and she knew she wanted to experience that same exhilaration again.

Every night since they had shared the bed at Mrs Barstow's farmhouse, Claire had relived her moments of rapture before going to sleep, but tonight as she tossed and turned in a state of turbulent anticipation Alan Jarvis appeared in her dream as a pragmatic prosecutor. When she woke with a start she felt as if she had been fighting for her life, and was in a turmoil of perspiration and panic. For the first few seconds of awareness she was convinced that she had not yet been to sleep, and in the next that she couldn't be awake, for there, silhouetted in the darkness, standing in front of the window, was the unmistakable figure of a man.

Claire felt her heartbeats pounding with fear, then she remembered Richard and switched on her bed-light quickly. He was poised at the foot of her bed and blinked at the suddenness of the diffused light. Claire was dazed too, but thankful that she had decided to wear a cotton nightdress with which she had originally intended to provoke Richard.

'Richard? Is something the matter? Are you all right?' she asked.

He dropped his face into his hands with an urgent: 'Oh, Claire!'

She was out of bed in an instant, her arms around him

comfortingly as she persuaded him to sit on the end of the bed.

'Richard, what is it?' she appealed softly.

'Darling,' he whispered, 'I've let you down so badly.'

'Me? Of course you haven't,' she insisted not sure of his meaning.

He put his arm round her shoulders and drew her close.

'But I have—I gave you to understand that this week-end was going to be a total eclipse——' He looked despairing.

'Let's go and make a cup of tea. Shall I fetch your pyjama jacket?'

He shook his head. 'No, thanks, but the tea is a lovely idea.'

He refused the kitchen stool Claire offered, instead he hovered behind her.

'You've been so kind to me, Claire, so good for me, and I can't even repay you.'

Claire turned on him then, the tea caddy in her hand.

'You don't have to repay me for anything, Richard. There's a lot more to it than that, isn't there?'

He spread his hands in a gesture of despondency, and was unable to meet Claire's questioning look.

'Let's take it into the lounge,' she said and prepared the cups on a tray while she waited for the kettle.

She switched on the imitation coal-effect fire in the lounge and let Richard sip the comforting beverage before pursuing the matter, then she asked gently: 'Can't you tell me about it, Richard?'

'There isn't much to tell, and I only want to say I'm sorry.'

'For what?'

'For letting you down. You're a normal healthy girl with a lot of sex appeal. You wouldn't have agreed to me staying with you if you hadn't expected us to sleep together.'

'Two people can share the same bed without committing any crimes,' she said in a low voice.

Richard looked up and smiled. 'You do it all the time, I suppose,' he mocked. 'Maybe you're not as normal as I thought. And who says sex is a crime?'

Claire considered her reply carefully. 'It is if one of the parties involved doesn't love the other or if either person is just using the other. I happen to be old-fashioned, Richard, and I do believe in love—not sex when it's merely an indulgence.'

'A noble philosophy, Claire darling—a pity more don't have your moral principles.'

'I'm no angel,' Claire answered. 'I'm not sure that I couldn't be persuaded in certain circumstances.'

'But it doesn't worry you in the slightest that I haven't attempted to?—how do you know that that isn't why I was in your bedroom?'

'Richard, she said patiently, 'you've been at Moorlands a fair time.'

'And I was a beast at the start,' he admitted.

'You were badly injured, alone and frightened—that's understandable.'

'But you didn't go for a soft touch, Claire, you deliberately tried to antagonise me—and it worked. I fell hopelessly in love with you.'

'But there's a wife, isn't there, Richard?'

'I told you there was once, there isn't now,' he said slowly, his face darkening.

'Where is she?' Claire asked determined to make him talk.

'South America.' He sighed, was it with longing or disenchantment? 'I made the mistake of marrying the boss's daughter.'

'How long?'

'Eighteen years.'

'Children?'

'Three. Seventeen, fifteen and eleven. Leaving them really hurt. I was sure my father-in-law would kick me out because I left South America before time, but he's been surprisingly understanding.' Richard grunted. 'Can't do without me really, I'm his partner—we built up his electronics business together. Thought going to South America would be fun, but it must have been the heat or something—my wife—I never thought she'd really be unfaithful to me. That's all there is to it, Claire. When I realised how far things had gone I decided to come home. She refused to come with me. If I'm unfaithful that makes me as irresponsible as she is, but—the way I feel about you, Claire—just give me time?'

'We all need time, Richard. I'm sorry about your marriage, really. Sex isn't a good basis for friendship, that has to be established first.'

She stood up and placed her cup and saucer on the tray. 'Now, let's get some sleep, shall we?'

Richard drained his cup, then stood up. He held open his arms and Claire went willingly into them. His body was warm but passive, a consoling shield for her slim and aching body. Not aching for Richard's passions, but those of a man whom she knew she could never have. A man she didn't want under the existing circumstances, but whom she knew was capable of persuading her with his magnetic charm. So, wasn't it the lesser of two evils to settle for a compatible friendship with Richard, if only to show Alan Jarvis that she could get along without his inducement and could readily refute his challenges?

As she settled down snugly in her bed, alone, despite Richard's suggestions that they do otherwise, Claire knew in her heart of hearts that she was making a big mistake. She was a fool to hope that by some miracle she could force herself to love Richard to the same degree that she did Alan. However much she tried to close her eyes and pretend, Richard's touch was not as thrilling as Alan's had been. But, she thought, Alan Jarvis would never have the satisfaction of knowing how much he had hurt her.

The following morning both Claire and Richard slept late and after a huge breakfast relaxed comfortably in the garden until the evening when they prepared to go out for dinner.

Claire dressed with care, her silvery blonde hair bouncy and shining after a shampoo. She wore a new dress in soft red crêpe which clung to the curvaceous moulds of her body, and from the provocative slit in the skirt one slim leg appeared from time to time to tantalise. A black purse in patent leather matched her very high-heeled shoes, and Richard expressed his appreciation of the trouble she had taken to please him.

But Claire knew that she had taken particular pains to look as devastatingly fashionable as Alan Jarvis's Fiona. They had met by chance at Lake Windermere, it was possible they might do so again at the smart restaurant of a lakeside hotel where Richard had telephoned a booking earlier in the day.

He was the perfect host, and after an aperitif they were shown to a small table in the centre of the huge semi-circular window which overlooked one of the many lakes in the area. It was a happy occasion as they ate pâté and roast duckling, followed by sherry trifle with lashings of fresh cream, all washed down with a superb French wine.

Claire's appearance attracted more than one surreptitious glance of admiration, but though she was alert to each new face entering the restaurant she saw no one who resembled Alan Jarvis.

When Richard's taxi was due to arrive next morning he said farewell to Claire in the lounge.

'It's been splendid and I feel ready now to face the world again. I can't thank you enough, darling,' he said and kissed her long and ardently before they recklessly planned what they would do on Claire's next weekend off.

Claire was grateful for the time to herself to prepare for work on the following day, but whatever she felt about what had, or had not taken place during Richard's visit the flat seemed to be full of him, and a pleasant aura surrounded her. Was it love after all? Perhaps infatuation for Alan Jarvis which had blinded her to her true feelings for Richard? Whatever it was, she felt more at peace than she had done for some time as she went on duty the next morning.

All the patients were pleased to see her back and she was kept busy with the many tasks which tended to accumulate when she was absent.

Claire decided to face Alan Jarvis with confidence when he visited the ward, but as it was one of his days for surgery he did a quick round while she was at lunch, so she felt she could relax. But when she went off duty and had kept her rendezvous in the shrubbery with Richard, she was astounded to find Alan Jarvis waiting in the car-park.

As she approached her own Fiesta he got out of the Granada and strode purposefully towards her.

'I want to talk to you,' he said fiercely.

Claire felt her cheeks tighten awkwardly, but she held her head high and with a confident tone said: 'Oh?'

He glanced around the car-park, now almost empty, and took a step closer to her so that he towered over her, and she could feel that magnetic power emanating from him. Inwardly she shrank from his influence, but outwardly she remained calm and seemingly indifferent.

'I thought I warned you about getting involved with a patient,' he said brusquely. 'Fancy putting your own telephone number in Mr Lynch's notes—have no you pride?'

'Of course,' she answered shortly. 'I'm surprised you

found time to check up on me, but ever since you came here you've constantly reminded me of my indiscretions.'

'So you admit them?—Claire, I'm really shocked at you. How could you behave so foolishly?'

'I've admitted nothing!' she said with venom.

His brown eyes were aflame with anger as he gripped her wrist.

'Are you going to try to tell me that there is nothing between you and Richard Lynch?' He laughed sarcastically. 'It's all so very touching—a trysting place in the shrubbery. That might be excused—like all women you're flattered by a little attention. But did you have to make yourself so cheap, allowing him to share your bed?'

Claire just stared at such audacity, but Alan gave her no time to speak up in self-defence.

'Blatantly going off together for the entire weekend. Kissing in the street—I thought you had more self-respect.'

'What's the matter with Richard, for heaven's sake? He's as good and honest as you,' Claire lifted her chin defiantly. 'More so by my reckoning. Who do you think you are, to preach at me?'

'I'm only trying to prevent you from being hurt.'

'But you don't care what *you* do for my reputation!' Her cheeks were crimson now as she recalled so vividly all that had happened between them. She had cherished the memory, but now could only use it to throw back in his face.

'You lied—to Mrs Barstow—cheated by not telling me how you'd implicated me—and then to creep into my bed when I was asleep! How much more despicable can you be than that?'

'Claire, you silly girl—what else could I have done? I'd told her we were married to get the room. Wouldn't she have thought it strange to bring us tea in the morning and find me in the chair? Country people are very hospitable. Besides, I enjoyed it, and if you tell the truth so did you.'

'But just one night spent together doesn't give you the right to tell me how to spend my off duty. Unless of course you're complaining about my behaviour *on* duty?'

He relaxed his hold slightly and his face drew very close to hers, so that Claire thought for a moment he was going to kiss her. But of course he wouldn't do that out in the open where some inquisitive onlooker might be watching—he had Fiona to consider.

'Claire, you're making a mistake—why can't you see that?'

'It has nothing to do with you,' she said bitterly.

'It has everything to do with me,' he argued heatedly.

'As you're a consultant, sir, as I believe I've said before, if you have any complaints there are the proper channels.'

'Claire, I am pleading with you as a man, as your friend——'

'You don't need to stoop to that,' she cut in sharply. 'You gave me a challenge to help Richard—that I have done. But there is no excuse for what *you* did, and I can never, ever forgive anyone who implicates me by lying and cheating.'

She tore her hand away, ran to her car and drove away with tears streaming down her cheeks.

CHAPTER TEN

CLAIRE was obliged to seek refuge in a quiet lane, where she blew her nose and dried her face before continuing her journey home.

Why did Alan Jarvis persist in antagonising her? What could it matter to him where or how she spent her free time? He didn't want to see her get hurt, he'd said. Didn't he know that *he* was the one who was hurting her?

She would have to get away from Moorlands, that was the only way to get him out of her hair. Richard was going to Scotland. Claire reasserted her determination and decided to get in touch with an agency who would find a position for her further north. She resolved that during her next weekend off duty, even if it was for only one day, she would press Richard into helping her arrange such a dramatic step. She was fond of Richard and he had confessed his love for her, so they might manage to set up home together and make it work.

But when the weekend came round Richard had developed a severe cold which affected his chest. He was put on antibiotics, and Claire was forced to spend Sunday afternoon and all day Monday alone, and when she returned to duty on Tuesday afternoon she realised with some disappointment that she would have to work for nearly ten days before the next opportunity would occur.

As she glanced through the double swing doors into the men's ward she saw that everything seemed quiet, and yet she sensed a hushed reverence about the place that was not usual on an operating day.

In her office she found Mike Boyd with Staff Nurse Jill Norris in earnest conversation, but they stopped speaking and broke apart as Claire entered the room. Mike trying his charms on Jill now, Claire thought vaguely as she greeted them cheerfully.

'Hi, Claire—good weekend?' Mike asked, patting her arm. 'Must dash—the boss will be back from lunch.' He rushed off, leaving Jill looking perplexed and annoyed.

'Hey!' Jill called after him irritably, but he had disappeared.

Claire laughed. 'What's up? Did he let you down?'

'No,' Jill said flatly, but her cheeks were dark red. She had a file of notes in her hand and she avoided looking at Claire as she toyed with the dge of the file.

'Whose file is that?' Claire enquired taking her place at the desk.

Jill Norris seemed reluctant to answer, but in a low voice replied: 'Mr Lynch.'

'How is he—better?' Claire said brightly, trying not to show undue interest.

'He's been discharged, Sister. He's getting ready to go now.'

Jill put the folder down on the desk and hurried away from the office.

Claire sat for a moment, thinking. Richard discharged? She could hardly believe it. Where was he going? Did he want the key to her flat?

She got up and walked into the ward, passing his bed, which had already been stripped, on her way to the day room.

Mr Wilson and Debbie were sitting together watching the proceedings and chatting to Richard, who was supervising the packing of a new suitcase.

Claire hesitated in the open doorway, shock and disbelief cutting into every fibre of her being as she observed the woman who was doing the packing. She was tall and well-built, with dark brown hair. 'A handsome woman' might have been a suitable description. The floral crimplene dress she was wearing was expertly cut and designed by a qualified dressmaker Claire could see at a glance, and when the woman looked up Claire saw that her face was beautifully made up with expensive cosmetics which toned down the deep sun-tan. She smiled at Claire, an easy but meaningless smile.

Claire willed herself to walk forward slowly but with authority, and although Richard lifted his head, he showed no emotion when he saw her approaching.

'So—you've been discharged at last, Mr Lynch?' Claire said steadily.

'Yes, Sister. This is my wife—just arrived back from South America.'

Claire acknowledged the other woman's presence as Mrs Lynch said agreeably: 'It's time I took my husband in hand and let you good people care for the really sick.'

'We are a combined hospital and remedial unit, Mrs Lynch,' Claire explained softly.

'We're very grateful for all you've done for him,' Mrs Lynch interjected, and Richard stretched out a trembling hand to Claire.

'You'll never know how grateful, Sister,' he said huskily.

Claire put her hand in his and he grasped it firmly. There was no need for words, because everything could be conveyed by the strength of his handshake and the clear liquid sadness in his eyes.

'This is what I tried to tell you, my darling,' came the unspoken message, 'but I still love you.'

Claire's courage was fading rapidly, but as Richard kept her hand in his she said in a professional voice: 'I hope everything works out well for you, Mr Lynch. I'll go and phone for a porter.'

She didn't say goodbye. Her heart was too full and she was thankful that Jill Norris appeared from somewhere, having already fetched a porter. Claire turned and walked briskly back through the ward, slicing the tension as she went, knowing that all eyes were on her, some condemning, some with pity, some with amusement.

She returned to her office, determined to ignore all conjecture. She sat quite still, Richard's open folder in front of her. It was a long time before she could bring herself to focus on the final report in his notes, and with a sinking heart she saw that Alan Jarvis had personally discharged him.

How he would gloat! Claire clenched her fists together on the desk. He could think what he liked, but she would never let him know that the suddenness of Richard's discharge had upset her, any more than she would reveal that his use of her had caused the biggest heartache.

Pride, Alan had said, and a challenge—well, this was the greatest challenge of all. To stay on at Moorlands and do her job efficiently, at the same time hiding her bruised heart from her colleagues.

Bruised because Richard had declared his love for her. A love which she couldn't reciprocate, a love which she felt convinced he was mistaking for a passing infatuation, and yet he had chosen to deceive her, even lie. Surely they must have been corresponding for his wife to come suddenly and take him home?

Claire was shattered too, because she knew that Alan Jarvis was the only man she could love with sincerity, and he was ineligible.

In the distance a bell rang, announcing the return of a patient from the theatre. Claire stood up, smoothed her damp palms down the sides of her apron and became Sister Claire Tyndall, dedicated nurse, with a duty to do for the patients depending upon her.

Inside she felt cold and weak, but she worked with a will of iron, refusing to concede to the sympathetic glances which were bestowed upon her. Only when it was all over did she realise the full impact of all that had happened over the last couple of months. She had not given much thought to what other people made of such friendships, and because Alan Jarvis had tried to deter her she had stubbornly refused to see it from his point of view.

No one spoke of it; in fact she almost felt as if she were being deliberately shunned by the rest of the staff. But that was because they expected—knew how hurt she must be feeling, so she had to show them otherwise. All the same, she was glad when eight o'clock came round and for once she went off duty promptly. She had to force herself to go through the shrubbery and when she reached her flat she flopped down wearily, realising how much she was going to miss Richard.

He would write, of course, to explain his sudden departure, but though she watched the postman eagerly every day no letters arrived bearing a Scottish postmark. One day he would telephone, and when such thoughts twisted and tormented her she became restless with longing. She had been prepared for a lecture from Alan Jarvis but he nodded curtly each time he visited the ward and kept the conversation to impersonal matters.

Claire knew that with every look he was condemning her for her stupidity. If he only knew, she thought, if he could look right inside my heart he would know that the most of my stupidity is in loving him. He would never know, of course. Claire presumed that his marriage to Fiona was on a more compatible level now. A nurse, and with theatrical interests Fiona would be highly emotional most probably, so that marriage to her would run a stormy passage.

Claire's spirits lifted each time the telephone rang, each day when the mail arrived at home or on the ward, but the fact that no word came from Richard urged her to go on living and hoping until the next day. But the days passed timelessly until she grew weary with expectancy and numb to her emotions.

Her flat still savoured of Richard's warmth, and her thoughts were instantly with him when she was faced with the sketches he had done of her in the garden, which she had pinned up in the kitchen.

She smiled at the reminder that he had considered her Eros a monstrosity. She wished that she were half as good as he had portrayed her, but she'd keep his sketches for ever as a reminder of a happy weekend. Through them she felt his presence with her.

Gradually as the days passed old patients went home, new ones came to take their places, and Claire found renewed satisfaction in her job.

Debbie Wilson was up and about and could have been sent home, but she was needed for company for her father as well as persevering to communicate with the still unconscious Mrs Wilson.

It was only after Richard's discharge that Claire appreciated how much encouragement Richard had given to the Wilsons. Richard and Mr Wilson were of a similar age and Debbie had been a constant reminder of his daughter.

Debbie had grown up during her stay in Moorlands, and once she was able to walk about freely had proved to be helpful. She liked to do things with Claire, sometimes assisting to make beds. She talked frequently about Richard, and Claire felt a pang of jealousy when one morning Debbie ran to her excitedly to show off a picture postcard of Buenos Aires in Argentina.

'He sends his love to you and everyone,' Debbie said, little knowing how the pain of Richard's indifference revived her memories of him.

Debbie pushed the colourful greetings card into Claire's hand, and when Claire seemed to be staring at it blankly for too long Debbie impatiently turned it over, pressing her to read the message. But there was nothing in it for Claire, not even a hidden word of affection—

simply 'love to Sister and all the nursing staff'.

Could he forget so soon? And why hadn't he said he was returning to South America? Claire read his message to Debbie several times before handing it back with a jaded smile. How could he have been so devious? Had this Scottish job been a pipe-dream? Was she so vulnerable as to attact men who used her, and then cast her off with never another thought?

Richard had said his wife had been unfaithful. Was it possible that some insane jealousy had caused him to see things which did not exist? Or was Mrs Lynch a dominant wife whom Richard had rebelled against, and then grasped an opportunity to escape her clutches? Claire's mind went back to her first meeting with Richard. His dark defeatism, his bitterness. Claire doubted that he had told her the real truth—now, she would never know.

When Claire saw Debbie greet Alan Jarvis during an early morning visit, showing him the card from Richard, Claire kept her gaze fixed firmly on the Kardex trolley. She sensed Alan's interest in how she was reacting, but she pretended to be engrossed in her patients' notes, and when he came to stand close beside her she thrust the first folder into his hand.

She felt him stiffen. She dreaded that he might be about to speak of Richard, but thankfully a junior nurse came to tell her that she was wanted on the telephone. She escaped to her office and was pleased to hear Mike Boyd's voice at the other end of the line, advising her of a new patient who had just been admitted and was on his way to the ward. By the time Claire returned to accompany Alan Jarvis on his round Debbie had gone to be with her mother, and she hoped that Alan had forgotten Richard.

Alan had refused all recent offers of coffee, except on one occasion when he and Mike were discussing a case in detail, but today he surprised Claire by accepting her invitation. Before they reached the office, though, Claire's new patient arrived, so she excused herself to see that the young man was comfortable. His injuries were multiple but not of a serious nature, and as he was still drowsy after being anaesthetised Claire left him to sleep it off, and she was returning to the office when she heard a commotion.

To her surprise the sound of hysteria was coming from her office and from the doorway, she saw Debbie clinging wildly to Alan's neck. Instead of attempting to disengage her arms Alan appeared to be welcoming her attentions. Claire just stood and stared, and then Debbie saw her and in a flash had thrown herself at Claire.

'Mummy's back—oh, Claire—she's back—she's really awake!'

Claire's upsurge of joy was equal to Debbie's.

'Oh, darling, I'm so pleased—that's wonderful,' Claire said, hugging the excited Debbie.

Alan showed his enthusiasm too by placing an arm around each of them, although Debbie was quite unable to keep still, and she clung to Claire and then kissed her before turning to Alan and kissing him too.

Claire felt a little breathless, not only from Debbie's exuberance but from Alan's touch. She had thought she was getting over him, but however lightly his skin touched hers it was like a spark of electricity which sent a current of excitement through every nerve.

'Will you come? Will you come?' Debbie urged, tugging at Alan's hand. 'And you too, Claire?'

Alan held Debbie's hands firmly in his and stooped to speak to her.

'Young lady—what is this I hear? Claire? She is Sister Tyndall,' he said severely.

'Richard always called her Claire—and I bet you do sometimes,' Debbie said flippantly, and he managed a look of familiarity towards Claire.

'I'm going to finish my coffee first, and Sister hasn't even had any of hers yet, then we shall be pleased to come and meet your Mum. But just listen to me, young lady. Calm down. If you're over-excited you won't be allowed in I.T.U.'

'Mummy won't need to stay there now, will she?' Debbie exclaimed, hardly able to contain herself. 'She'll be in my ward, won't she?'

'We shall have to do lots of tests and things now, Debbie, but we're all happy for you. It's going to be a new beginning for you all, isn't it?'

He held Debbie's chin in his hand and forced her to look at him. His words sobered her at once. Not that he meant to dampen her spirits, but she had to be reminded that selfishness can cause unhappiness for others. Debbie had been laughing and crying at the same time, now she was weeping gently.

Alan tickled her under her chin.

'Come on now,' he whispered. 'You mustn't spoil that lovely face.'

Debbie pressed her hands fiercely against Alan's cheeks and through her tears she faced him bravely.

'I love them both so much,' she whispered back and then she left them, Alan looking after her with affection, and Claire with a lump in her throat.

A subdued silence stretched between them until Alan turned Claire round to the coffee tray.

'Have your coffee now, Claire,' he said in a low voice, and then he turned and left the office. She had the feeling he had been going to say a great deal—perhaps about the Wilsons, or the new patient—perhaps about Richard. One day he was going to mention him she knew but for now he had deferred his inquisition.

Before she went off duty Claire visited I.T.U., and was delighted to find Mrs. Wilson taking an interest in all that was going on around her. As Alan had told Debbie, there were still tests to be carried out, investigations to be made and great care to be taken, but Claire had a feeling that things were going to be all right for the Wilson family from now on.

It was good to feel happy for them, but where was the happiness Karlotta had predicted for her? It wasn't often that Claire indulged in self-pity but sometimes, just sometimes when Richard's name was mentioned, or Alan Jarvis came close to being nice to her, it seemed as if her universe tilted cruelly. Usually after a good night's sleep everything came right side up again, but once Debbie had received a card from Richard, Claire's hopes of a letter from him were revived again.

But why should he write to her? she asked herself savagely as she prepared her breakfast. He owed her nothing. Hadn't he warned her that there could be nothing for keeps between them? If only he hadn't spoken of love. She hadn't really believed him then and she didn't now. It had all been just a flash-in-the-pan for him. He loved his wife, had done all the time, and probably their weeks of separation had only served to strengthen the tie between them.

Claire knew she was well rid of him. Such a relationship, however mild, could only lead to unhappiness, she told herself for the umpteenth time as she drove to Moorlands. She was still trying to convince herself of this when Mike Boyd called into her office at midday.

'You're going to help on Saturday, aren't you, darling?' he greeted.

'You never bother me unless it's to ask for something,' Claire retorted good-naturedly.

'I bother you? Good, then that means you will.'

'I'm on duty all day on Saturday, *Dr Boyd*. Open Day at Moorlands is a spit and polish occasion, and I shall be too exhausted to help at the barbecue. Besides, I thought the catering staff were going to do all the barbecuing this year so that the nursing staff could eat and have fun.'

'Yes, that's right, but some of the younger members of the medical staff want a dance as well, so we thought some of your Quiche Lorraine would be nice. Couldn't you and Miriam get together? You're such experts, Claire,' he pleaded.

'You've got the cheek of old Nick,' she said. 'Have you asked Miriam?'

'Yes, and she's willing, but then she'll do anything for me.'

'I bet,' Claire scoffed.

'I'll dance every dance with you, darling,' he promised.

'Big deal!—I shall be home in bed.'

'Come on, Claire. Don't be a spoilsport—you know what a good partnership we are,' he goaded.

She flicked him with the menu card.

'Go worry someone else,' she admonished. 'I'm not available this time.'

He made a grab for her, holding her tightly, bending her backwards and with a Charles Boyer accent declared his love for her, teasing until she was helpless with laughter.

'You are a fool, Mike,' she said in mock anger, setting her cap straight.

'At least I made you laugh, darling, and no one's done that of late. You never know, someone might come along and sweep you off your feet—but if you don't come to the barbecue and dance you'll never know.'

'That's a risk I'll have to take, then, won't I?' she said as she hustled him out of the office. 'My patients are ready for their lunch, Dr Boyd.'

'And I'm ready for love,' he sang as he skipped off.

Claire smiled, knowing that as always she'd do whatever Mike asked of her. Not to please him, but because she always did, and along with Miriam actually enjoyed helping to make Moorlands Open Day a success.

The weather had always been kind to them on previous occasions, could it be again this year? Gladly she woke on Open Day to see the sun filtering through the clouds. Perhaps it was better not to be too brilliant first thing, the clouds might clear later, and by mid-morning when all the dignitaries and local clergy had arrived for the ceremonial opening, only a few cotton-wool buds were left spotting the blue sky.

Claire and all the staff were required to be on duty all day, but fitting in relaxing periods when they would take part in the festivities and mingle with the patients and their visitors in the grounds.

The wards were all sparkling clean, with fresh flower decorations in abundance, and Claire, while tending the less active patients, some confined to bed still, was on hand to talk to the V.I.Ps and visitors, explaining in detail the work of her particular unit.

They came in droves at intervals throughout the morning and afternoon, led by the Senior Nursing Officer and the various consultants, registrars and housemen.

Alan Jarvis and Fiona had accompanied the Mayor, whom Claire had met on previous occasions, and who greeted her cordially while Alan and Fiona looked on with some amusement. Mike followed that party with some of the local clergy, and Miriam seemed to be excelling herself escorting a team of local G.Ps. There was never much time to talk to anyone for long, and Claire was kept busy seeing that all her staff had an opportunity to go into the garden and circulate, or try their luck at hoop-la or skittles.

There were stalls of every kind, and earlier when Claire was leaving home she had walked through her small garden to the garage and had caught sight of her Eros. Richard had laughingly called it a monstrosity, so with a sudden impulsive whim to be rid of the past she had picked it up and returned it to the white elephant stall from where she had originally acquired it. Now at five o'clock and with her first chance to walk in the grounds, she made her way to the stall again, regretting her hasty action of this morning, hoping to retrieve her Eros.

It was true he hadn't greatly influenced her love life over the last year, but if she didn't keep him her fate might be even less eventful. The stall had all but sold out and there was no sign of her Eros. Somehow she hadn't the courage to ask about him, so she moved on to the refreshment tent feeling disappointed. She tried to shrug off fatalistic thoughts, and rebuked herself sharply for allowing herself to become involved in astrology and superstitions, wishing she'd never met Karlotta.

Among the throng of people trying to get a cup of tea, Claire suddenly felt an arm pushed through hers and found Debbie at her side.

'You've missed all the best bits,' Debbie said. 'There was a lovely exhibition in the hydro-therapy pool, and afterwards Mr Jarvis and Dr Boyd took on two patients at table tennis in the Gym.'

'Who won?' Claire asked.

'The patients, but I'm sure the doctors let them win.'

'It's all for fun, Debbie, and think of all the new equipment the hospital can buy from the proceeds.'

They moved up in the queue and as they procured their cups of tea Claire looked about for a vacant table and came face to face with Fiona Jarvis.

She looked immaculate as always, wearing a flimsy voile dress, heavily flowered and multi-coloured. Her black hair was elegantly styled and she was wearing the usual large, tinted spectacles. Claire didn't imagine for one moment that Fiona would remember her, but she was edging towards Claire in the crush.

'Hi there—aren't you Alan's little dolly-bird that hurt her leg?' she greeted.

Claire hoped the shock of hearing an American accent didn't show, and as she was jostled at that moment, nearly losing her tea, she was unable to reply.

'How's the leg?' Fiona drawled.

'Fine now, thanks, it was nothing,' Claire said.

Fiona looked her up and down.

'I'm surprised Moorlands hasn't gone in for a more modern uniform—I mean—well, darling, forgive me, but you do all look a bit Florence Nightingale.'

Claire bristled. Now she was certain that she didn't care for Alan Jarvis's wife, but she managed to smile.

'New uniforms were designed, but we took a vote on it and this old-fashioned style was preferred almost unanimously.'

'Quite unacceptable in the States,' Fiona said, then looking down at Debbie she added: 'And of course, you're Alan's little heart-throb, aren't you? I hear your Mom is making great progress.'

Claire wondered how Debbie was going to react when a hearty voice greeted them with enthusiasm.

'Why, Mrs Jarvis—I knew I'd find you here somewhere. How are you, my dear—and your leg?'

Claire felt her body go cold and the hairs on the back of her neck prickle. Even Debbie was stunned into silence.

Mrs Barstow was talking to Claire! What could she say—that it had all been a terrible mistake?—she hardly dared look at Fiona but when she did, the American girl took off her sunglasses, glared with open hostility towards Claire, and with a toss of her chignon turned on her heel and pushed her way out of the marquee.

'Mrs Barstow—how nice to see you,' Claire managed at length. 'I'm fine, the leg healed up very quickly,' she added hastily.

'I haven't seen your husband anywhere yet—but my goodness, what a crowd! It's very hot in this tent but it's a lovely day—heaven sent, my dear.'

'I ... I must get back now—have a good time, Mrs Barstow,' and Claire desperately tried to disentangle herself from Debbie's stranglehold. She was jumping up and down with glee and when they got outside the marquee she faced Claire excitedly.

'You're blushing,' she accused. 'Fancy *you* being Mrs Jarvis all the time—you lucky thing,' she prattled on.

'Debbie, it's not like you think—it was a mistake—that lady made a mistake.'

'I don't believe you—hey! Where are you going, Claire? You've only just come outside to join in.'

'There's a lot to do, Debbie, you carry on enjoying yourself.'

'All right, *Mrs* Jarvis,' and Debbie giggled cheekily.

Claire looked for the shortest route back to her office. God, what had she done? Now Fiona would really be able to confront Alan with first-hand knowledge of his misdemeanour, and he'd be furious with Claire. Then there was Debbie—she was going to tell the whole world. How on earth could she shut her up?

Claire watched every minute pass for the next couple of hours desperately wanting the time to come for her to go home. Any minute Alan and Fiona had to come to challenge her to the truth. How would Alan get out of it?— the truth was too naïve for words. Fiona would simply never believe him!

There was so much tidying up to do that a quarter to eight arrived without her realising it, and the night staff came on duty a little early so that the day staff could prepare for the evening's jollification. But that was not for Claire. She only wanted to hide herself away and hope she never had to face Fiona again. She hardly felt fit to drive herself home, but when she did reach the block of maisonettes she put her car away thankfully and shut herself in trying to forget, but knowing that she wouldn't ever forget such embarrassment. First there had been Richard's wife to face, now Alan's—dear God, was there no end to this charade? she pleaded.

She had only one thing to be thankful for, and that was that she had taken all her pastries to the hospital kitchens that morning. No one would miss her. She could take a handful of aspirins and simply opt out for the next twenty-four hours. Perhaps after that things would not look so black.

Claire wandered up and down in her flat unable even to put the kettle on. Alan would be livid; she could imagine the terrible row there would be between him and Fiona, but it was all his fault. All the same she wouldn't have had it happen for the world—jolly Mrs Barstow would never know what she had done.

By the time it grew dark Claire had managed to make a pot of coffee. Her head ached, her eyes burned, not from weeping—what use would that be?—but from strain. She felt physically sick knowing that now she would be obliged to leave Moorlands. There would be gossip—Debbie would already have started that—but for Alan's sake she would have to go miles away where her name could never be connected with his again.

She must telephone her father. A few days in London might help her to think and plan more clearly. She was so deep in thought that the bell which echoed through the flat led her to the telephone, but she hesitated before answering it, and then the front doorbell pealed ominously again.

She couldn't imagine who it might be at this hour so she called nervously: 'Who is it?'

'Open this door, Claire, it's me, Alan,' came the stern command.

All kinds of stupid notions flooded through her brain,

and only his persistent banging made her slip back the bolt and undo the catch.

The hall light was dim and Alan peered at Claire, his eyes skimming over her in disbelief.

'You're still in uniform, Claire,' he observed in surprise.

'I couldn't help it, Alan—what could I say?—Mrs Barstow just appeared.' Her voice began to shake, and because he remained so calm she let all her fury and fear explode in near hysteria.

'It was all your own fault,' she yelled. 'If you tell one lie you have to tell a load more to get out of it. You cheated me, you made up the story—it wasn't my idea. What did you expect your wife to say if she found out?' The words kept flowing, all Claire's anguish came pouring out until Alan held her arms tightly and shook her until her teeth rattled.

'Stop it!' he shouted. 'For goodness' sake be reasonable.'

'Be reasonable!' she repeated as he slowed down, and the effects of his physical restraint made her lift one foot and stamp it down in a last attempt to avenge her confusion. Her foot landed on his. He released her at once, all colour draining from his face.

'Claire!' he said, the pain emanating from his voice.

She quickly covered her mouth with her hand, and Alan as rapidly recovered and held her arms again savagely.

'Now listen to me, you—you—oh, Claire, why must you be so tiresome?'

'You can't blame me for your domestic upheavals,' she said.

He sighed impatiently.

'Let's begin at the beginning. Fiona Berkeley is *not* my wife,' he explained. 'Fiona—is—a—very—bad—habit,' he spelled out slowly and deliberately. 'Correction—

Fiona *was* a very bad habit.'

'Fiona is not your wife?' Claire repeated guardedly.

'No, darling, she is not—nor really was ever in the running. Not from the moment I joined the staff at Moorlands, that is. Oh, she came home from the hospital today and accused me of two-timing her—convinced you and I'—he shrugged—'but she has no claim on me. She didn't fit in at Birchdale either, so I'm glad to say I've just seen her off with one of her theatrical friends.'

'But she's a nurse, isn't she?' Claire asked lamely.

'That's right—so what? Her main interest is the theatre—she doesn't need to work. She's hounded me since we met in New York. We sort of—no—*I* was never convinced we could make a go of it, and I've been certain of that since *we* met, *Mrs* Jarvis.' He smiled. 'Wouldn't you like to make it official?' he asked softly.

Claire wasn't taking it in. She babbled on trying to make him understand that Debbie had been present—that Debbie would by now have told numerous people.

Alan gave up, then noticed the coffee pot on the side and poured her out a cup, then took a cup from the rack and poured himself one. He rattled the aspirin bottle. 'You won't need these, now stop talking and drink,' he ordered her.

She did as she was told, and followed his gaze to the sketch of her posing naked with Eros. She rushed forward to snatch it down, but he stopped her, smacking her hand sharply.

'Where did you get that ornament?' he demanded.

'I haven't got it now,' she said. 'I bought it last year at the white elephant stall at Moorlands. Today I took it back—then wished I hadn't.'

'Why?' he questioned solemnly.

Claire shrugged. 'I . . . I suppose I wanted to get rid of it because it reminded me of Richard—and at the same time I wanted it back—probably for the same reason.'

'You're not really over Richard?' He took her cup away and made her look at him.

'Was there anything to get over?' she asked Alan simply.

'You tell me.'

'He said he loved me——' she began, as if that explained everything.

'But you, Claire—I want to know *your* feelings?'

She didn't answer him at once, but her blue eyes regarded his features with a passion that surely spoke for itself. He wasn't married to Fiona—she was a bad habit, he had said. Claire could barely take it in, let alone come to terms with it.

'Don't you know how I feel?—have felt for weeks?' she whispered softly.

'I want you to tell me. Tell me that whatever was between you and Richard is all over—really over, Claire—no hang-ups.'

'I never loved Richard because I love you,' she blurted. 'Like you said out there on the fell, I was flattered by his attention. I felt sorry for him, I wanted to help him.'

'And when his wife showed up?' Alan prompted.

Claire looked away. 'I didn't think that Fate could be so cruel, nor did I think Richard would reject me with just one clean sweep of his brush.'

Alan's eyes switched back to the sketch on the wall.

'He's made some very fine sweeps of you. He's very talented,' he conceded.

'It was just for fun.'

'You forget, darling, I know the real thing.'

She blushed, remembering, and Alan tilted her chin, then laughed softly. 'Shall I tell you a little story about that ornament?'

'My Eros?' she asked with a frown.

Alan nodded. 'He's at home, in the garden at Birchdale, waiting for the new Mrs Jarvis.'

'You bought him?' Claire asked incredulously.

'I bought him back. He's part of my inheritance—he belongs to Birchdale. When my grandfather died, some well-meaning busybody gave him to Moorlands. I wanted him back, hoping he might have some influence on my future love-life.'

'You're sending me up again,' she said disbelieving him.

'Come and see for yourself,' he invited sipping his coffee. He rinsed his cup at the sink. 'Time we were at Moorlands, or all the eats will have gone.'

'I'm not going,' Claire said flatly.

He swung round from the sink, and pointed a warning finger. 'You may not have vowed yet to love, honour and obey, my girl, but we may as well start as we mean to go on.' He pointed to the hall. 'Do you want some help? A quick shower—and wash all memory of Richard Lynch away while you're there. Hurry, I feel like dancing.'

'But how can we face everyone?' Claire asked helplessly.

'Who's going to spoil our little deception? As you so rightly said, darling, one lie leads to several more, and who knows that we *aren't* married?'

'But ... b ... you *can't* do that—we'll never get away with it!'

'You mean you don't want to marry me?'

'Oh yes, yes,' she cried, suddenly afraid that she was going to lose him.

'So what's to stop us pretending that it's already happened? Oh, I expect you want to have a posh family affair with all the frills. Well, your folks are in London—mine in Scotland, but they'll be delighted to travel to London for the biggest event in the Jarvis family since the year dot.'

'Are you an only child?' she asked.

Alan nodded. 'Yes, and I've never minded, but I expect I'm spoilt and selfish, so you may as well get used to the idea that I like my own way. Now, move, we've got the rest of our lives to exchange family gossip.'

Claire ran to the bathroom, suddenly realising that her world had made a miraculous turn about. She showered happily and then discovered that all she had to protect her modesty was a not-too-large towel. She opened the door as quietly as she could and emerged cautiously when Alan's voice called from the lounge:

'I found some sherry and I've poured you one.'

'I'll dress first,' she answered preparing to make a dash across to her bedroom.

'Come here!' He came to the doorway and beckoned her to him, so she decided it was best to go meekly.

He enclosed her in his arms and kissed her, intoxicating her with his own style of impetuosity for a few ecstatic moments before he sent her off to dress.

Claire chose a particularly feminine dress in a soft shade of emerald green. It had a satin finish which shimmered as she moved and Alan's eyes opened wide in appreciation when she pirouetted for his approval. The style gave her height as it clung to her slim form in figure-hugging precision. The bodice was merely a scarf which crossed and covered each breast, leaving her back bare. Where the two ends of the scarf joined a narrow waistband it left a provocative diamond-shaped space, and the skirt was only mildly flared, allowing the satin to fall in rippling folds.

'You look lovely,' he complimented as he escorted her to the door, 'but it'll be time to take it off before we even get there if we don't get a move on.'

The barbecue was in full swing when they arrived at Moorlands Park and had been for over an hour. There were hamburgers, beefburgers, sausages and pork chops to accompany sizzling brown chips. Coloured lights were strung out from tree to tree and lit up the beautiful parkland, from where, in the distance, the white buildings which clustered together to form Moorlands Hospital and Remedial Unit could be seen.

Claire was hungry, and was soon tucking into a plate of sausages and chips while Alan went in search of some wine. There was a great atmosphere of congeniality among the staff and when they had eaten they moved into the huge marquee now being used as a dance hall.

Mike waved to them from a distance with Miriam, who, with a pork chop in a serviette, was returning to the hospital and her duties. There would be much more frequent and short working shifts throughout the duration of the festivities, but for Claire and Alan there was nothing to hinder their enjoyment, and almost at once Alan took Claire in his arms to waltz her around the marquee. A few minutes later, to a smoochy serenade, he clasped his hands around her waist and drew her even closer.

'People are looking,' Claire whispered.

He answered with a long, lingering kiss and gently forced her head against his shoulder.

The sensation of being so close to his masculinity carried her into a dreamy world of mystique, and she found herself considering all that had happened. Alan had talked now of pretending they were married. But she was not wearing a ring, so what chance had they of fooling anyone? He had been quick to suggest the type of wedding they would have, but was that all a pretence too?

Richard had deceived her, but that was unimportant because she didn't love him. What Alan did or said mattered because she loved him—but did he love her? The realisation that he had not said so brought a stab of pain to her heart. Was he only pretending again after all? Playing games with her, just as he had with Fiona? Did he lie and cheat her as well? Claire was suddenly shocked to realise that he was only using her to get rid of Fiona, and when he'd done with her—what then?

She pulled away sharply from him and he gazed down at her with a puzzled frown.

'I want to go home,' she said, her blue eyes full of mistrust.

'Darling—what's the matter?'

A last tug released her from his embrace and she walked as sedately as she could towards the opening of the marquee, knowing that Alan was following in her wake. Her mind was filled with terrible thoughts, but she willed herself to remain dignified as she wove her way through members of the staff and their friends until she was well clear of the marquee.

'Darling—where are you going?' Alan called, but Claire's eyes were misty with disillusionment and she began to run, bent on getting away.

She lifted her skirt and set off across the grass, dodging between trees, breathless because she was crying, and then strong arms restrained her and roughly forced her against a large oak tree.

'Claire—what have I done? What's the matter, for God's sake?'

'Don't you know?' she screamed at him. 'Lied, cheated, and utterly fooled me—you used me just to get rid of Fiona, I suppose. What imaginative engineering you went to, to get Mrs Barstow to appear just at the right moment.'

'Stop it at once, Claire!'

'You won't need to marry me once you've got everyone believing we are already married,' she accused angrily.

'Claire—what are you saying? I love you—though God knows why, you stubborn little egghead—I love you—crazily—and all I want to hear is that you've forgiven me for what I've done to you.'

He pulled her away from the tree-trunk, one hand

magically touching—caressing her neck as his lips sought and toyed with hers until she was forced to open them for breath, and then his tongue coiled itself around hers.

His hot and demonstrative passion quelled her fears, and his loving touch tenderly wooed her back to sanity. His hands slid over her bare back until she relaxed, and after the relaxation came the response when her mouth craved for more of his kisses, and she waited breathlessly for the moment when his exploring fingers edged their way beneath her dress to fondle and stimulate the skin which tingled over her throbbing heart.

'Oh Alan,' she sighed, 'is it really true? Do you honestly love me?—enough to marry me?'

'I love you with all my heart, darling,' he assured her, 'and we're married already.' He kissed her ardently, sealing his vow, and in the distance the church clock struck twelve. His mouth fluttered over her neck and shoulders and settled, enthralled, in the hollow of her bosom.

'It's Sunday, sweetheart—and you're always going to spoil me on Sundays.'

Claire linked her arms around his neck, willingly accepting his challenge, loving the feel of his skin against her soft fingertips, and she looked upwards to the stars and smiled.

'The most ineligible man is making me supremely happy,' she told the universe.

Doctor Nurse Romances

Don't miss
October's
other story of love and romance amid the pressure
and emotion of medical life.

ATTACHED TO DOCTOR MARCHMONT
by Juliet Shore

Doctor Sally Preston's relationship with her new chief, Darien Marchmont, got off to a sticky start. So she was less than pleased to discover that their first joint assignment was a two-man medical survey in the heart of the North African desert!

Order your copy today from your local paperback retailer.